The Serpent Finder

The Serpent Finder

A tale of mayhem and intrigue, high finance and low cunning

by

Peter H Fowler

Copyright © 2000 by Peter H Fowler
All rights reserved.
No part of this book may be reproduced, restored in a retrieval system, or transmitted by means, electronic, mechanical, photocopying, recording, or otherwise, without written consent from the author.

ISBN: 1-58820-343-3

1stBooks - rev. 9/22/00

To my patient wife.

Chapter 1

"We should go out and catch it." With these innocent words Joe caused all the trouble, though he now denies ever saying them.

It all started as we were sitting on my patio looking out at the Pacific, waiting for the sunset. It was attitude adjustment time, the time when we use drinks of one sort and another to blend the stress of the day into the turmoil of the evening. Tonight though we planned no turmoil, just some idle wondering where to go for dinner.

The sea rippled with the dying waves of the Pacific, furrowed with the wakes of small boats scurrying back to the marina before the sun went down and their captains needed real seamanship. My friend Joe, the mystic of our group, spoke.

"Maybe we'll see the sea serpent."

There was a long pause while we thought about this remark, unconnected as it was with anything said previously.

"What sea serpent?" asked somebody who should have known better than to encourage Joe.

"You know, sailors are always telling about the Santa Barbara Channel sea serpent, claim they see it all the time."

Somebody got up and poured refills, feeling I think that we were going to need them. We sipped for a while in silence. Curiosity eventually overcame prudence and I asked, "What does this alleged serpent look like, Joe?"

"Well, I haven't actually seen it myself," a rude noise came softly from some skeptic among us, "but it's the traditional serpent, like in the old pictures, you know, squirming up and down."

I hastened to put Joe right. "Not a serpent then."

"Of course it's a serpent, what do you mean?" Joe was quite indignant, afraid I was spoiling his story.

"It can't be a serpent if it squirms up and down, reptiles only bend from side to side, they can't move up and down. Haven't you ever seen a snake?"

There was another long pause, broken only by the sound of ice being pushed to one side to get at the healing virtue of the drinks.

Blake stepped in, with an air of surprise that I'd said something sensible.

"He's right. Reptiles can't bend up and down."

Joe was now feeling the effects of one too many scotches-with-not-too-much, and getting belligerent.

"Alright smart guys, in that case, what the hell is that out there in the channel? Can't bend up and down can't it, the fuck it can't."

We tried to focus into the setting sun, to see what Joe was talking about, if anything. There was certainly something moving out there, something long and sinuous and . . . serpentlike. I mentally reviewed just how many drinks I had actually had; maybe it was a few more than I realized. A glance round the group reassured me, their rapt attention and the even more telling fact that one of them dropped his glass, indicating they could see it too.

We watched as whatever it was sank from sight in the glitter of the setting sun on the waves. I came to first and suggested, "Let's go to dinner."

Five is tight in my Mercedes, so Blake elected to take his flat red car, which, the rest of us felt, was tight for one, and descended on our favorite Chinese restaurant. A girl smiled at Blake as we walked through the parking lot, so we were four for dinner as he opted for turmoil.

I ordered the specialty of which I am very fond, seaweed and baby oyster soup. It tastes like the sea. By tacit agreement we refused cocktails and stuck to hot tea, afraid we had already had more liquor than we could handle. After the eggroll stage, as we started on the four dishes on the lazy susan in the center of the table, conversation made a hesitant start. William (he hates to be called Bill) asked for opinions as to what we had seen, and got no coherent answers. Joe had evidently given the matter careful thought, fueled by the pre-dinner drinks. He spoke.

"We should go out and catch it."

I called the waiter over and told him we had changed our minds, bring drinks. The five of us had tried some fairly esoteric adventures, but this promised to be a new experience. Chasing a non-existent animal round the Pacific. We munched on crispy duck, Mongolian beef, seafood noodles, or something I wasn't sure what it was, as our appetite suggested, thinking about Joe's proposal. I added what, in this group, passed for a practical suggestion.

"We'd need a real boat, something solid, not my yacht. I know where there's an old seventy foot tugboat hull been half converted into a yacht, needs a little work but it has a new Cat diesel."

Three pairs of eyes focused suspiciously on me. They had some previous experience with projects of mine which 'just needed a little work.'

"Where, just where is this boat located? Not Alaska again, you know how that turned out."

I remembered very vividly how that turned out, and it hurt to be reminded of it. In any case, the only financial loss was mine and I could afford it. Only a sissy makes such a fuss over a simple broken arm, so I don't know why they have to keep bringing the subject up.

"It's in Winchester Bay, Oregon," I told them.

Mike wanted to know where Oregon was, evidently having missed it somehow. I reminded him it was the stretch of little fir trees which separates California from Washington. The group wanted to know why anybody would go to Oregon to get a boat when we had lots of them in California. I explained.

"For a start, all the boats I know of here are flimsy things, not suitable for chasing monsters. Look what happened when I let Blake borrow my last boat, who would have thought just hitting a little thing like that would have sunk it? We need something sturdy, with a nice thick hull. Besides, there's no sales tax in Oregon, that'll save enough to do the work on it."

As it was taken for granted that I was funding the enterprise my view prevailed, though the three of them had dire predictions as to the probable outcome. Pessimistic lot, my friends.

After dinner and the imaginative claims for what the fortune cookies had in them, we went back to my house for more drinks and some plans. We didn't expect to see Blake again, but he reappeared about eleven-thirty with an air of grievance and a strong reluctance to talk about his evening. We settled down to make real plans, with the Chivas handy as an aid to thought.

Blake had to be briefed on our new enterprise, promptly entered enthusiastically into it on condition no women were invited for the trip. The rest of us agreed in the certain knowledge that by tomorrow Blake would have changed his mind. No minor setback was going to affect his rampant sex drive for long.

We sat making progressively less practical plans until after midnight, at which point Blake said he wanted to be alone and went home to a chorus of warnings not to get another DUI as he wouldn't get off so easily a second time. The rest decided it was too much trouble to go home, and Joe was already fast asleep in his chair, so we distributed ourselves among the various beds, settees, and floors available and slept the sleep of the innocent.

The cold light of dawn, if you count ten in the morning as dawn, brought a less enthusiastic frame of mind. Coffee with just a drop of brandy in it restored something like life, and slowly brought back the power of speech. The suggestion of breakfast was treated as if it were an invitation to supper with the Borgias, so we sat quietly drinking coffee and regretting the last few drinks of the night before.

"We aren't really going looking for an imaginary monster, are we?" William sounded worried.

"It's not imaginary. We all saw it." Joe was sticking to the story.

I had given it some hazy thought, and regretfully poured more cold water on Joe's story. "There really couldn't be animals that large living out there in a busy channel. The navy, the coast guard, about a million amateur marine biologists, TV channels with helicopters, it's impossible, somebody would have noticed. Sorry, it sounded like a good idea last night."

"Then what did we see? Answer me that, don't pretend there was nothing there, Mike even dropped his drink." Joe had a point, though I thought the liquor could have something to do with it. Still, we couldn't all have the same hallucination. And to my recollection it certainly looked like a serpent, but with the setting sun on the water who could be sure?

"Then," Joe said with an air of reasonableness, "we should go out there and find out what it was. We can afford it."

This brought out a chant of our group mantra.

"The Tyro International short squeeze."

"Ten million shares at eleven."

"On margin."

"Sold at sixty two weeks later."

"And one hell of a lot of income tax to pay."

The margin account was mine, but the others had contributed to the capital so none of us were in any danger of starvation, though as I'd put most in I got most out. Of course, I wasn't exactly starving before this coup, but there's comfortable and there's rich, and I like rich.

"Well, if it's real, let's brainstorm what it might be, before we go chasing off after something foolish." The group wanted to know when that had ever stopped us, but I reminded them this was going to take serious money and cut into our raising hell time.

"I bet it's something of the navy's." A sensible contribution from Mike.

"In that case, do we know anybody in the navy?"

Blake volunteered. "I know a navy captain."

We all stared at him, because this seemed unlikely.

"She comes up here once in a while from San Diego. We see each other." That explained it. "I could ask her."

So there was our first action item. William had a question.

"Wouldn't something like that show on all the sonar everybody uses?"

Joe answered as our expert on matters technical. I should have explained that Joe worked as a design department manager in our largest local aerospace company before our little windfall, and now owns a small custom electronic design firm. Which, I might add, he rarely visits except to solve problems in the design area and argue with the accountants. There he manufactured, improbable as it sounds, computer controlled smart traffic light control systems. He sold most of them abroad of course.

"Sonar doesn't give a real picture, though there have been some attempts to sell devices that give a synthetic perspective view. They take too much computing power for a commercial device, and can't give a real picture because of the limitations in the transducer."

Now who was going to argue with this? Whatever it meant, we were sure it was right. Any question I asked was going to be a silly one, so I dived right in.

"Joe, why aren't there underwater holograms, like optical ones but using sonar?"

This produced a long pause while Joe muttered to himself and somebody poured more coffee. With a little more brandy. Eventually Joe spoke.

"I think you could make a sonar hologram, but there is no way to record it, and it wouldn't display . . ." His voice trailed off and he went into a trance. We resumed normal conversation around the oblivious Joe, knowing he would return to us eventually to say something we wouldn't understand.

We moved out onto the deck to survey what of interest might be sunning itself on the beach. Suggestions for lunch were greeted with a little more enthusiasm than breakfast. We decided on the yacht club, partly for the food and partly to see if we could get some opinions on local sea serpents. In a casual sort of way of course. So we scooped up Joe and piled into my car and off to Marina Del Rey.

We ordered what we thought Joe would like, which he ate without coming out of his trance. Conversation and drinks flowed round him while he looked into some distant electronic landscape closed to the rest of us. We had more or less forgotten about him when, during the coffee and liqueur interlude, he spoke.

"I'm not sure it couldn't be done. Illuminate the scene with a chirp like whales and dolphins use, record it in a pair of hydrophone arrays. Might be able to recreate it optically using stacks of liquid crystal displays. Might work, have to try it."

I asked the key question. "How much Joe, and how long to do?"

"I'll have to go down to the plant and talk to the guys. Not long, maybe a year and about a million dollars."

"And," I asked as the probable banker for the enterprise, "it *might* work?"

"I've never heard of anyone trying it. We'll need a real computer, not a desktop. Something from Sun I expect. I could probably tell if it would work in a couple of months, with a boat to test it."

If it were just a matter of chasing imaginary sea creatures I would have dropped the project right there, but . . . if Joe could do it there just might be a substantial profit opportunity in it. I could dimly see a lot of interesting things it might be useful for.

"Joe," I asked, "If we use my yacht are you going to damage it or upset the insurance company in any way?"

"Oh no, just drill a few holes in it, no problem."

"No holes. I'll buy a little barge to tow and you can drill all the holes you like in that. And Joe, everything you come up with gets a patent application, understand? Everything."

And that's what we decided to do, insane as it was. I'd fund Joe to demonstrate he could build a monster watching sonar, and if he could we'd equip an expedition to search for one to catch. And incidentally demonstrate the commercial possibilities.

Chapter 2

So Joe disappeared into Mico Electronics, which is what he calls the collection of sheds in Torrance where actually he does make some money. On the infrequent occasions when we saw him it became clear that he was neglecting the normal things in life, like eating, sleeping, and washing. I thought we should find a capable housekeeper to look after him, so ignoring Blake's suggestion as unhelpful I selected a professional housekeeper from the agency I used to help recover from the various minor domestic emergencies that crop up. I interviewed several before selecting a pleasant middle aged woman whose manner I thought was the right combination of practical nurse and drill sergeant. We installed her in Joe's condo without him apparently noticing, and his appearance improved markedly.

With Joe taken care of and working well I went looking for a barge of some sort for him to experiment on. I couldn't find a barge, but I found an old thirty-five foot cruiser in poor shape that could be adapted. I had it towed to the yard for a little work. The dead engines were removed, the resulting holes plugged, and a 10KW diesel generator substituted. The cabin doors were reinforced and fitted with a more authoritative lock. Marine plywood was bolted over the windows for security. The interior was stripped and workbenches with florescent lights substituted for the cabin furniture, but I left the galley, head, and forward bunk in place so the necessities were taken care of. I had them add a reinforced bitt to the bows so I could tow it without it falling apart, and there was Joe's marine laboratory. He was delighted with it when I dragged him away from Mico to see it and had his minions start fitting cryptic machinery and instruments to it. As an afterthought I had them add air conditioning, as there were no windows any more.

It didn't tow worth a damn by my new bitt, shearing wildly from side to side to the entertainment of the lookers on, so we lashed it alongside my yacht with plenty of fenders and kept to an unaccustomed sedate pace. My dock is an end tie, so I thought it would be hidden from the officials of the club, but apparently some nosey and officious members living in the condos along the front complained that it wasn't a yacht and lowered the tone of the place. I had rather a tiresome interview with the dockmaster about it. He seemed skeptical of my explanation that we were helping The Institute (carefully unspecified) with a project on the ecology of the bay.

"And this had better not bring down another Coast Guard raid," was his parting shot.

Now I have explained repeatedly to him, and to the Commodore, that the friendly information gathering visit by a Coast Guard detail, which we inadvertently triggered, was not in any sense a raid, and anyway some of the ladies of the club had told me how much they enjoyed it. "The most excitement round here since the Commodore's boat caught fire," was what one of them confided to me in the bar after it was all over. Actually this was rather an unfortunate thing to mention, as he had cherished an entirely unjustified suspicion that I had something to do with that incident too.

Joe worked for three months before he was ready to try his enterprise at sea. Our entire group wanted to come on the trip of course, so I reminded Blake of the standing rules about any friends he might invite. "Blake, remember. No incurable diseases, no herbal cigarettes, not even crumbs at the bottom of someone's purse because the coast guard is still into zero tolerance, and topless is OK but panties are required." I don't know what it was about Blake that all his lady friends had in common a compulsion to take off their clothes if the word "party" was even mentioned. They also had in common the belief that "boat" and "party" are synonymous.

There seemed to be a lot of people on the dock ready to take part in the sea trials. Joe and two assistants disappeared into the laboratory, and the rest crowded onto the yacht. I warmed up the diesels and thinned the crowd in the pilothouse down to the point I could get at the controls, then sent Mike to cast off. We edged slowly through the marina and out of the channel to the open sea much hampered by the laboratory alongside and the maniacs in small sailboats. However, we got out without actually colliding with anything, turned out of the north entrance, and headed into the Pacific. Mike went to ask Joe how deep he wanted the water, and came back with the message that Joe wanted us to cast him loose when we got in four hundred feet of water. I didn't think freeing Joe to float alone in the big sea with no engines and no way to see out was a very good idea, so trailed him behind on a long rope and headed very slowly towards Japan.

I noticed two topless girls sunning themselves on the foredeck, wearing what might pass for panties apparently made from a piece of string and some ribbon. Oh well, near enough I suppose.

With the autopilot taking care of our heading I went out to see what Joe was up to. He and his crew were busy rigging booms from the sides of his laboratory, trailing door-size masses of equipment, connected by a bundle of wires as thick as my arm through the cabin wall and out of sight. Their free and easy approach to drilling, screwing, and nailing things up the way they wanted them confirmed the wisdom of my decision not to let Joe use the yacht for his laboratory. I hoped the extra bilge pump I'd had put in would keep them afloat if they drilled holes in the bottom.

The day wore on, coffee and sandwiches came and went, drinks circulated in the salon, and everyone seemed to be enjoying themselves. Belatedly I realized I should have given Joe a radio. Along about four in the afternoon he appeared and waved to me. I stopped the boat and started to haul him in, but his frantic hand waving indicated that was not what he wanted. I pointed to the dinghy, and he nodded vigorously. I swung the crane out and dropped the Avon into the water, left Mike in charge of the boat, and motored back to see what Joe wanted.

"I think we may have something," he said as I climbed aboard his laboratory. "Come and see."

I was expecting something along the lines of a CRT display with some sort of sonar trace on it, but that was not what Joe pointed to. I was looking into a black box whose sides sprouted wires all over. Inside the box was a faint background glow, and suspended in the middle was a school of little green blobs swimming about. They weren't on a screen of any sort; they were just there. As I watched they swam out of the green glow and vanished.

"Those were fish," I said in amazement.

"That section was from about a hundred feet down, the best I can do with this equipment. I think it may be possible to develop this to a useful size," Joe said thoughtfully.

"Joe, you've done a miracle, invented something completely new. I never imagined anything like this. Can you make it bigger?"

"I think so, still needs a lot of work though."

"Let's go back to the boat, these two," I indicated his assistants, "can join the party and you and I can talk."

William, who is in the legal business, Joe, and I spent next morning with the most expensive patent attorney we could find, planning how and when to file for what. We wanted to cut the system up into unrecognizable pieces and make the patents separate so we had as long as possible before anybody realized what Joe had done. Then we went on to another law office and started on incorporating the 'Mela Ocean Survey Company,' named after a character in a series of my favorite books. Joe and I took the majority shares, me because it was all my money so far and Joe because he did the work. The other three fellows got some for coming up with the question, and we saved some for the help later on.

Joe settled happily down to develop the Serpent Finder, under proper adult supervision at home, which I must say he didn't seem to have noticed. Now we needed a real survey vessel. I contacted Jerry Frank, the yacht broker who tries to keep me out of trouble when buying and selling boats. He greeted my request that he start negotiations for the old tug with ribald amusement, under the impression this was another practical joke of some sort. I persuaded him I was serious, so he reluctantly arranged to meet the listing broker in Winchester Bay.

I called my usual travel agent and asked her how we got a party of five to Winchester Bay Oregon. I didn't believe her at first, thinking even the airlines couldn't send us to Portland to get back to North Bend, the only airport near where we wanted to be. When I understood the ramifications of a journey into the wilds of uncharted Oregon I told her to charter a plane for us for the day so we could go straight to North Bend, instead of three hundred miles north and then back three hundred miles. Besides, a private charter plane is much more civilized than commercial air travel these days.

We arrived in due course at the marina, and trooped down the dock to the end where the boat lay. She was an imposing sight, looming over the little effeminate plastic boats around her. She had the low black hull and jaunty, slightly disheveled, air of tugs everywhere. The flowered curtains at the windows added a touch of color contrast to the white upperworks. Her almost new Cat diesel was reassuring, and her sturdy build looked just right for what we needed. Not pretty mind you, and fairly primitive. The chain drive direct from the steering wheel to the rudder, snaked through a considerable distance of pulleys and pipes, was particularly impressive. The instrumentation consisted of a radio of antique design, a compass which might have been a museum piece, and a new rev counter. Nothing else.

"How about hauling her so we can see what's underneath?" I asked the broker.

"Nearest place that can handle her is Coos Bay, where you came in. I can see about arranging it, but we'll need a crew."

I took Jerry aside. "What should we offer for her as is, no survey, no questions?"

"You are out of your mind," he protested, "she's almost a hundred years old."

"Never mind, see what he'll take for cash here and now, a check on the spot."

So we became the proud owners of a seventy-foot converted tug of uncertain parentage. Now to get her to Wilmington to start work on her. We walked across a parking lot and a small headland to look at the exit from Winchester Bay, which I knew wasn't very deep. We stood in silence contemplating the boiling mass of foam and breakers that lead from the harbor out to the wide Pacific. We could see there was every chance that our adventure would only last a few minutes no matter how sturdy the old boat was.

"How," I asked the broker, "do we get out of that?"

"Oh," he said cheerfully, "that's quite calm, no problem. You should see it when it's rough. Just wait for the slack high tide and power through it."

Easy for him to say, he wasn't going with us. We arranged for the tanks to be filled, oil and water, and went home to think about it while the title transferred.

We held long earnest discussions, studied charts and the coast pilot, to reach a plan of action. Joe, we thought, should stay home. The trip held every prospect of being prolonged and stressful, time better spent working. Also, the majority ruled against Blake that this time NO GIRLS. He muttered about it until we actually got out on the ocean, then changed his mind and joined the majority, but that came later.

When we judged the weather, tides, and our spirits were right the charter plane took us back to North Bend. The Fred Meyer's in Coos Bay provided canned food and a few cases of light refreshment, which with our duffel bags and my two hand-held GPS receivers filled two taxis to Winchester Bay. I settled up with the harbormaster, we loaded our gear, and looked for places to sleep. Below decks there was plenty of room, though the accommodations were mostly bunks rather than real beds. Not the style we were accustomed to, but not bad. There was a handsome new name painted on the stern, the "Mela Mermaid" of Portland, Oregon.

As high tide approached I warmed the engine and called the US Coast Guard to inquire what they thought of the entrance conditions. The young man was very helpful, in his way.

"Oh yes, I think you can make it alright. Give us a call when you get out so we know how it was."

I felt that fell a little short of the reassurance I needed, but as usual we set boldly off into the maelstrom in the quite unjustified faith that there's a providence which watches over drunks and lunatics.

That chain driven rudder took considerable effort to operate, so I had worked up a pretty good sweat in the few minutes, hours it felt like, it took to get to the end of the channel and out to sea. The last breaker at the entrance sent a shower of spray right over the pilothouse and we were free. Seven hundred miles to go with chain steering and no autopilot.

Chapter 3

Steering this boat with a chain turned out to be as onerous a job as I'd feared, with four days and nights to go before we could get it out of the water and rebuilt properly. After an hour I passed the helm over to William and went on an inspection tour of the engine room and inner spaces. I re-emerged with an announcement to make.

"Fellows, I've decided we're going to live in Coos Bay Oregon for a while."

"Why," they wanted to know, "might that be?" That was not precisely how they phrased it, but the meaning was there.

"Because there's two feet of water in the basement and I don't know where it's coming from."

I called the Coast Guard again. "This is the seventy foot 'Mela Mermaid.' We have a slight emergency here-we seem to be sinking. We're about ten miles out between Winchester Bay and Coos Bay. How is the entrance, assuming we make it?"

They went through the usual ritual of asking how many on board, were we wearing life preservers, and said they'd send a cutter to escort us in. In due course it came bounding up and kept us company into Coos Bay, through an entrance only slightly less alarming than the one we'd left. There is a really capable shipyard there, which had us dripping on the land in no time. Just as well – the water inside the boat was getting quite deep.

It was obvious where the leak was. The ten tons of water we'd been carrying came pouring back out of the shaft log seal, dry and perished from lack of use. The yard people seemed to know what they were doing, so I made a quick decision. We'd do some of the refit here.

My crew mutinied, as they had determined that the area offered for entertainment only an Indian gaming hall in a disused lumber mill. There also didn't seem to be any restaurants of the caliber we were used to, and no yacht club for us to stay at. I put Blake and Mike on Alaska Air for Portland and wished them well.

Repacking the seal took no time, but I wanted more. I had them convert the steering to a modern hydraulic system, coupled to a really capable autopilot. A modern suite of instruments made the trip look a lot more comfortable, new bottom paint and some minor hull work made it safer, and a new refrigerator and freezer added to the amenities. The bill was a bit of a shock, but I'm sure less than it would have been in LA.

When the boat was back in the water and successfully tried out I called my crew to return. William had developed other plans so couldn't come, but three was more than enough for a crew now. It took them two days, owing to their having met some people on the plane to Portland who invited them to stay. I rather chafed at the delay, because I had now tried every restaurant for miles around and the motel wasn't what I'd call luxury accommodation. I should have known I couldn't let Blake off the leash by himself without his getting entangled with some girl, and Mike was no better.

The power steering and modern electronics made the boat a pleasure to pilot, so we spent most of the trip relaxing in the sun. Four pleasant days later the Mela Mermaid was pulled out of the water again in Wilmington, ready for a few small changes.

The yard foreman and the marine architect walked through the boat with me full of enthusiasm, planning I think to send their children through college on this job. I wanted it plain and utilitarian, no mahogany no frills, still the estimate came to quite a lot of money. Five staterooms with their own baths, a new cabin on the stern for Joe's equipment, upgrade the galley, and repair some wear and tear, ran well into five figures. Plus some extra for doing it in a hurry. I also specified that Joe's laboratory on the stern should be tied right down to the ribs and capable of taking a sea over the stern.

Three months later we took her to her new dock in San Pedro, where she wouldn't offend the yacht club, ready for Joe to fit the Serpent Finder. The arrangements for raising and lowering the great flat transducer arrays (Joe's name for them) alone added appreciably to the boat yard college fund.

Our first trip, a shakedown cruise, was to be down to San Diego, up to Monterey, and back to Wilmington. In preparation I interviewed Joe's keeper Judith to tell her she was no longer needed because Joe's absorption in his invention had come to fruition. I anticipated a rather difficult meeting, but she was all smiles and sweetness about it, agreeing with everything I said. I noticed she was younger than I had thought when I hired her, some difference in attitude and perhaps her hair was new. I'd thought she was in her thirties, but late twenties seemed more like it. I got the impression that she found what I was telling her amusing, which I couldn't understand. I could see she might be happy to be finished with the job of trying to keep Joe neat and fed, but why should my laying her off be amusing?

After endless delays we finally got free of the dock, crowded with well wishers, at dusk. The boat seemed to have a lot more people on it than the five of us who belonged, Blake's doing no doubt. I shooed everyone out of the pilothouse to work my way through the channel and out of Angel's Gate, then settled down for a nice busy time avoiding freighters and oil islands until I could set the autopilot for a clear run to San Diego. Joe took the first watch on the Finder. Our plan was to do four-hour watches, two at the helm and two at the finder, ready to push the 'record' button if anything interesting appeared in the magic box.

Everybody crowded round the finder when Joe turned it on. There was an awestruck silence as a beautiful clear view of the sea floor and some fish appeared in the box, moving slowly by as the boat moved. These sonic holograms are commonplace now of course, but seeing one for the first time is still a significant experience. Looking into Joe's box was like being a giant peering in at a miniature world, one in which sea serpents might appear at any moment. Certainly all sorts of junk showed up on the sea floor, sunken things and interesting unrecognizable objects. This looked to me like one of the great inventions of the new century.

After my spell at the finder I went to the galley to get some supper, then down to my stateroom for some sleep. I was startled rather than surprised to find a girl in my bed.

"Hello," I said, "what's your name?"

She lifted the bedclothes slightly to give a glimpse of what was within.

"Does that really matter?" she murmured.

Put that way I guess not.

Some three hours later the alarm marked the start of my next watch. I freed myself from what felt like a warm damp octopus and took over the helm. Nothing needed attention, so I went to the galley to get a snack. I found it occupied by a woman dressed in a very elegant robe, a lot more modest than what I expected to see on one of Blake's friends but all the more fetching for that. Clinging curves, if you know what I mean. She welcomed me with a smile and offered a sandwich. She looked familiar, but I couldn't place her for a moment. Then it dawned on me.

"You're Joe's keeper!"

"My name's Judith and I'm Joe's guest, if you don't mind."

"Oh, no," I hastened to assure her, "happy to have you aboard. Are you helping with the Serpent Finder?"

"No, I'm just keeping Joe company."

That explained her attitude to being laid off. She had adopted him. Or he her.

I finished my watch in thoughtful mood, wondering just how this match I had inadvertently created would work out. Mike relieved me at the Finder, freeing me to return to my bed where my new friend seemed very glad to see me. I began to wonder if I had the stamina for a week of this sort of voyaging.

The day watches were more informal, so we didn't always get the same times up at night. When I got to bed near midnight I was disconcerted to find a new girl in my bed. Really, Blake was overdoing the entertainment on this trip.

"What's your name?" she asked as I started to get undressed.

"Does that really matter?" I asked.

Apparently it didn't.

The third night produced a different experience. As usual I found a delightful girl in my bed, but when I got up to take the midnight watch she asked if she could come and keep me company, got out of bed and put her slippers on. She even told me her name, Pam.

"Thank you, yes, I'd appreciate that," I told her in some surprise as neither of the previous girls had showed what you might call a personal interest in me, "but put a robe or something on, you'll get cold like that." Undoubtedly ornamental her birthday suit but not suitable for a night watch.

Only a cave could match the utter dark of a cloudy moonless night at sea. The instrument lights turned down as far as they go become uncomfortably bright once ones eyes get adjusted. Pam looked out of the windows into the utter black.

"You can't see anything, how can we rush along without headlights?"

"I could turn the searchlight on, but it would just dazzle us. There's nothing to see. If there were another ship close it should have lights, but sailboats often don't. I can see with the radar. Anything big enough to bother us'll show on the screen, and if the computer thinks we might collide it'll sound a warning beep, getting louder and faster as we get closer. But the sea is so big a lot of crews don't even bother, they just all go to bed and leave the ship to run itself."

Then we had one of those rare experiences that the sea gives to make up for all the cold, wet, frightening times. Suddenly the sea lit up gold shot with brilliant blue flashes. The blank black now let us see deep into the water rushing past, mysterious with colored lights and dim movement.

"Oh, oh, what's happening?" gasped Pam.

"That's phosphorescence, millions of little shrimps making love. You don't see it often along this coast. Quite a sight, isn't it? Go out of the door and look at our wake, should be exciting."

She opened the door to a rush of cold air and leaned over the rail to look behind us. We were leaving a boiling river of fire on the sea, stretching away behind us full of green and gold swirls. Then the ultimate gift appeared. A tribe of dolphins came boring through the gold in green tunnels shot with blue. They wove intricate patterns of fire under and round the boat, reveling in the pleasure being alive in such a place. You can't appreciate the true grace and joy of life of dolphins until you've seen them playing in phosphorescence, shooting past, diving suddenly out of sight twenty or thirty feet down still brilliantly outlined. I grabbed Pam's robe to stop her leaning over the rail too far.

"Oh, I just want to jump in and play with them," she said. "It's so beautiful it's making me cry."

"Oh hell," I said, "the engine raw water screens'll be all full of shrimp puree."

The second half of the watch, at the Finder, fascinated Pam almost as much, though she couldn't watch the picture for long because the sway of the scene in the opposite direction to the roll and pitch of the boat made her feel giddy. She waited the whole of that two-hour stretch with me though. Back in my nice warm bed she did her best to show how much she'd appreciated the experience.

The serious business of the trip went splendidly. The Finder worked flawlessly, and we recorded all sorts of interesting things in the sea. Sunken ships, boats, airplanes, mystery objects, seafloor which didn't match the charts at all, no end of interesting things. The high spot was our celebrated movie that caused so much excitement later of a nuclear submarine moving at a speed and depth that the navy would rather have kept to themselves. Many marine creatures, but no serpent. Still, the Finder was obviously going to be a huge commercial success if we could keep it for ourselves. History has too many examples of great inventions from which the inventor gained nothing. The cotton gin for one.

On the sixth day, as we headed back to Wilmington, I took Blake aside with a question now bothering me.

"Blake," I asked, "every night on this trip so far a new girl has appeared in my bed. Don't think I'm not grateful, especially for Pam. It's been very educational, I don't know where you find them. One thing puzzles me. Joe brought his own, which none of us expected. I've entertained five ladies so far. We only have five staterooms, so one has been left over each night. Where did she sleep?"

Blake looked embarrassed. After some prodding he explained. "Nobody slept alone."

"Blake, you are amazing. I think we should donate you to medical science. Do you mean to say you entertained *two* of them each night? And kept the same watches as the rest of us?"

"Well," he admitted modestly, "some of them were tired and just wanted to sleep."

There were chores when we got back. Empty the boat of girls, luggage, perishables, garbage, and a stack of full computer discs. See that everyone went home. Except the blonde Pam, who wanted to stay with me as she claimed to be temporarily homeless. I told her I would be happy to offer her a temporary home, and I was. I liked her, and she thought I provided memorable nights. Hire a security service to watch over the Mela Mermaid. Store some computer discs in a safe deposit box at a bank I don't normally use, in case anyone outside might want them. Not that they could read them without one of Joe's machines.

Next day we held a meeting to decide where to go next. It was interrupted by a telephone call bringing trouble.

"This is agent Jones with the Federal Bureau of Investigations. We want to talk to you about your using stolen classified government property."

"This is a joke, right? Who is this really?"

"I assure you this is no joke. We have reason to believe that you and your associates have used stolen government designs to build some sort of advanced hydrophone."

"Rubbish. Any designs we have are our own, the government had nothing to do with them. Anyway, how do you know what we've designed?"

"That attitude will do you no good. However, we are prepared to discuss the return of the plans to the SQV Corporation from which your associate stole them."

Now I understood what was going on. SQV wanted our designs, which we hadn't been very careful about keeping quiet. They were trying to use the government to get them by claiming a security violation. Not the first time it's been done. Better hear what they had to say, with William present. And some other arrangements.

"OK, come and see us at my place this afternoon and we'll talk about it."

We all gathered to receive them, including Judith who Joe seemed to be relying on for a lot of decisions. Pam sat in with us, though she really had nothing to do with the matter. When the doorbell chimed she jumped up and escorted two government men in. We could tell they were from the FBI-they were almost identical in appearance, and wore light gray three-piece suits like uniforms. It crossed my mind that Pam's action was a bit odd, but I forgot it in the excitement of the meeting. When everyone was settled and we had carefully checked their identification, I opened the discussion.

"What possible reason do you have for thinking the design we're allegedly using for an alleged hydrophone has anything to do with SQV or the US government? Any design we may be using Joe did from our suggestions, long after he left SQV."

Agent Jones answered. "I'm afraid the story that he developed a new device just won't play, we don't believe it."

"Joe," I informed them, "has a doctorate in physics from MIT, which is more than you do."

"Well, perhaps," he answered with a smirk, "they have their quotas too. Everybody knows his sort of people don't invent things."

Judith put her arm across Joe to restrain him while I answered this.

"Do you mean to sit there and tell us you don't think Joe could have designed something new because he's black? Is that what you're saying?"

"I wouldn't have put it quite that way, but since you ask, yes."

"You must be out of your minds," I told them. "What do you think a court would say to that?"

"We are here to talk about your returning the designs to SQV, if you comply the courts won't come into it. If you don't you'll be subject to arrest, and we'll have the plans anyway."

William as our attorney spoke up. "This is in fact a blatant attempt by the government and the corporation to steal our design, and illegal from start to finish. You haven't any evidence to back up your claims, the courts will throw it out summarily."

"Perhaps," the other agent answered, "but you people will spend time behind bars while we search your homes and businesses for the plans."

I decided it was time to take the offensive. "Fortunately," I told them, "everything said since you came has been recorded.

I'm going to send copies of the disc to our Senator and the NAACP, see how your department likes that. You can't have the plans, and I assure you there are no copies at Mico or any of our homes. Now get out of here and tell your supervisor we expect an apology if he doesn't want more publicity than he can stand."

"We'll go and get fresh instructions, and we'll be back with warrants next time. Think about it and don't do anything foolish, you're in enough trouble already."

With which they left, leaving us to stew over it.

Chapter 4

Judith released Joe, who had a lot to say and did he ever say it. I don't blame him, being insulted by government agents on both a personal and professional level. We sympathized and let him run down.

I was about to open a discussion of what we should do next when Judith suddenly spoke up.

"Pam, we're almost out of Chivas, and these fellows look as if they're going to need some. Would you be helpful and take the Mercedes down and get a few bottles?"

Pam was very reluctant, but eventually left with a handful of money and the keys. "What," I asked Judith as the door closed, "was that all about?"

"There's a leak somewhere, and it's not me. We don't know anything about Pam." Blake looked at me and sniggered and was glared at. "I thought it was safer if she doesn't hear any more."

I remembered her eagerness to answer the door when the agents came. "You might be right, doesn't hurt to assume she's a pipeline to SQV or the FBI."

An inconclusive discussion was in progress when Mike spoke up.

"I have a suggestion, if you'd like to hear it."

We assured him that we'd listen to anything that might help.

"What we need is a powerful friend and public support. Suppose we got Geographica to sponsor some sort of research trip. We could keep it quiet, leave without drawing attention to ourselves, then get the results published so the FBI would look even worse if they tried to steal Joe's work."

"What about the discs of the FBI insulting Joe, what do we do with them?" I asked him.

"Mail them after we're gone. By the time we get back the fuss will have died down and the government will be on the defensive."

The meeting agreed unanimously that Mike's idea was brilliant, and as the editor of Geographica was a woman Judith was nominated to invite her to a demonstration of the serpent finder. By charter plane at our expense.

Now we had to decide on a destination. A possibility occurred to me, but Pam came back laden with elixir so I told Mike I'd brief him in private so only the two of us knew what we were planning.

We went for a walk on the beach with our drink, fairly generous with just a little soda and in my case no ice. I laid out the plan that had occurred to me. Mike liked it, but had a concern.

"Isn't that rather a long trip for that old tug? Across a whole ocean? Through the Panama Canal? It would be the perfect project, but it must be almost ten thousand miles. Geographica should just lap it up, but not if we sink on the way. Couldn't we find something as good here on the West Coast?"

"The Mermaid's engine is almost new, and she's been refitted at vast expense. I don't see why not, she was intended for the open sea and we can pick our weather."

"Let's try it on the others, without details, and without Pam."

We told the others only that we were heading out soon on a several months trip for which they would need passports. William had a problem with that.

"I still have some clients, and I think as the attorney of the group I should stay to protect our interests."

I didn't argue, because that emptied a stateroom for Geographica if they wanted it. Pam was looking worried, as she had realized a trip was planned and she hadn't been invited yet. I put the question to her.

"How would you like to go on another yachting expedition?"

"Yes," she said with a relieved smile, "so long as I only have to sleep with you."

Out of the corner of my eye I saw Blake look a bit taken aback by this, which raised my self-esteem quite a lot.

"Have you got an up to date passport? In case we visit Baja?"

She produced a nice new one, which added to my slight concern about her. But it was after all only an insubstantial suspicion and she was fun to have around. And interesting in bed.

Provisioning the Mela for the whole trip would have been rather conspicuous, perhaps precipitating some action by the FBI to stop us. Instead I suggested that Judith and Pam might like to take my credit card and provision the boat for a couple of weeks, so it looked as if we were sticking to this coast. In private I arranged with a ship agent for fuel and provisions at Balboa on our way. With a reservation for a stay at the yacht club and for a pilot through the canal.

Another difficult chore was to persuade Blake and Mike that this trip was not to be some sort of orgy. For one thing we didn't have room, and for another I hoped to have a Geographica crew with us.

"Two girls between you and Mike, Blake, and no arguments. We've got to act reasonable and fairly respectable. Judith doesn't share, and Pam doesn't want to, so you two make any arrangements you like in private. And remember we're going for months, though Pam doesn't know that, so if you bring guests think about getting along for a long time at sea. Try and find girls who do something useful, like cook. And they must have passports."

Blake wasn't sure he wanted to go under those rules but he and Mike went off to see what they could work out. In a couple of days they produced quite a good choice, a pair of sisters named Mary and Leah. Both claimed they could cook, and both had some yachting experience and could stand watches. While I wouldn't say they were an inconspicuous pair, they weren't quite as spacey as some of Blake's friends, and dressed relatively modestly. On land anyway. Leah in particular struck me as a cut above the usual run. They had met them at the health club instead of a bar, which made them different right off.

Judith had been very persuasive on the phone, promising the Geographica editor an experience well worth the trip. She had clinched it by supplying my credit rating. The coincidence that the editor's name was Judy didn't hurt either. Joe and Judith and I met the chartered Lear jet at the west terminal, then continued on in the same plane to John Wayne airport, which lost the people who had been diligently following us from when we left the house. By the time they found us again we hoped to have editor Judy back on the plane and gone without a trace.

In the taxi ride back to the boat at Wilmington we explained the expedition we planned, suggesting she send a crew with us, either from the start or meeting us at one of our ports of call. She wanted to know what was so special about our "underwater survey system" otherwise known as the Serpent Finder, but we told her the demonstration was all she would need.

Once on board the Mela Mermaid, which impressed her as a capable sea boat and no toy, Joe warmed up the display unit and started playing discs for her. The results were everything we hoped for. We showed her sunken ships, whales, and the climax – a nuclear submarine whizzing by. She was astounded.

"It isn't a trick of some sort, is it? It's unbelievable. Can I touch them?"

She put her hand into the viewer. The picture vanished in an amorphous green glow, to reappear when she took her hand out again.

"If you like," I told her, "we can take the Mela out and let you see it live, but then you'll have to stay over and go home tomorrow."

"I'd love to, but I don't have time. You really mean we can have an exclusive first publication on this?"

"With a couple of provisos," I warned her, "we must have absolute confidentiality until the story actually issues, and you have to send the writer and photographer for the expedition. If you've got someone familiar with the subject it would be better."

"Can I see the accommodation?"

We showed her the stateroom now reserved for them. I added another proviso.

"Also, if you send a couple we would really prefer heterosexual, as anything else would be disruptive. We need to keep the crew balanced."

"No problem, I've got the perfect pair. Mikel and Natasha. They're married, he's the photographer and she's our middle-east archeology expert. You can photograph those marvelous pictures?"

"Oh yes, but of course they won't be holograms in the photo. You could do 3D plates in the magazine with colored spectacles folded in, but that would be very expensive and I don't think you've ever done it before. We were planning to leave soon, when can they join us? Come on the charter jet tomorrow would be ideal."

I could feel my credit card squirming at the prospect of what this was going to cost.

"That's too soon, how about they meet you at Balboa?"

And so it was decided. We took her back to the airport and watched her disappear into the evening sky. Now for our getaway.

We set about leaving in the most casual way we could assume, obviously not hurrying and making no secret of our plan to go west to Monterey and have another look at the seafloor there. I made a point of waving to the car that followed me about, which seemed to annoy the occupants. We straggled on board in the late evening. At the last moment I 'remembered' to run up to the dock office and remind them to keep our slip open, as we'd be back in a few days.

We slipped out of Angel's Gate in the setting sun, and turned to go west up the coast. I deputed Mary and Leah to take fenders in, stow the mooring ropes, and tidy the deck, to see how they would operate. Apart from a certain amount of squealing and giggling they did a capable job, boding well for the rest of the trip. Once past Santa Monica I turned towards San Diego, on our ostensible short cruise. I told Joe not to set the hydraphones, because I was afraid of running into some debris with them and spoiling the trip before we got started, and because the drag used some extra fuel. Three watches carefully avoiding oil islands, barges without lights, sailboats with inadequate radar reflectors, and all the other minor hazards of the coast in this stretch, brought us to the Customs station in San Diego as they opened for business in the morning. We cleared for a voyage along the Mexican coast still with an assumed air of nonchalance and left around lunchtime at leisure.

Clear of the harbor mouth I headed straight out to sea, setting the navigation computer to head two hundred miles straight out before turning towards Panama, avoiding the Mexican navy with it's well deserved reputation for extortion from large yachts.

The Mela at reasonably economic cruise did nine knots – flat out just under eleven, so a normal day's run in calm weather is just over two hundred miles, or for you landlubbers two hundred and thirty statute miles. The voyage to Panama is a little over three thousand statute miles, twelve days motoring. Several tons of diesel oil. We would have to be careful with the food, but of course the engine driven watermaker would keep our tank full of desalinated sea.

Once in the open sea watches can be fairly relaxed, as there's very little chance of running into anything. The radar would sound an alarm if anything big approached, so there was no need to stay in the pilothouse. I went on a tour of the boat to see how everything was doing. The engine was happy, nothing leaking out of it and no vacuum on the fuel filter, the shaft log was almost dry as it should be, and nothing heavy was loose waiting for a big wave to project it at someone Excellent but for a minor problem. I found Blake watching DVDs in the salon.

"Blake, where ever I go on this boat I seem to find naked women. The rules haven't changed, topless is OK but pants will be worn, and not string ones either."

He wanted to know why as we were all alone out here.

"Because it's better for the upholstery and for peace and tranquility. We can always go back and put anyone ashore who can't live with that."

He set reluctantly off to establish order in the harem.

Pam appeared in the pilothouse as I handed the watch on to Mike.

"Where are we? Where's Mexico?" She wanted to know.

"We're going a little further than that, our next stop is at the Panama Canal."

"The Panama Canal! Why are we going there?"

"To get to the Atlantic."

"Why on earth should you want to go to the Atlantic?" A touch of hysteria sounded in her voice.

"To get to the Mediterranean."

You're teasing me, right? It's a joke, we're going to Encinada, right? Why would we go to the Mediterranean?"

Chapter 5

To say that Pam was miffed when I convinced her I meant it would be a definite understatement. Spitting mad would be closer.

"You asshole! You got me on this boat for a week and now you say we're going to the Mediterranean? You're out of you're fucking mind, you let me off and go on and drown yourselves in this old wreck." She went on in this vein until she ran out of breath and stood breathing fire and glaring at me.

I had prudently taken a step back out of range of nails and teeth so made a vain attempt at a conciliatory reply.

"It's a secret, it's essential that nobody knows where we're going. You might have done something to give it away, and we couldn't risk it. You were anxious enough to come on a nice yachting trip, it's just going to be a shade longer than you expected. Besides, where do you want to be let off? We're two hundred miles out to sea for the next three thousand miles."

This speech did not sooth her appreciably.

"Take me back to San Diego, right now."

I refused, pointing out several cogent reasons. I evaded her attempt to slap or scratch, I'm not sure which and she stamped off down the companionway, presumably to lock herself in my stateroom. Oh well, I could sleep in the pilothouse. Get some needed rest too. And if she was a spy for SQV she was now out of touch.

I really got quite a good night's sleep, hardly disturbed by the changes of watch. One of the watches appeared as a pair and objected to my occupying the bunk, but disappeared again on my assurance that I would look after the boat. This I did for four hours of deep sleep, with every confidence in the innumerable warning devices glowing softly round me. This sleeping alone has a lot to recommend it, at least occasionally.

Full daylight and the bustle of people wanting breakfast roused me to face the problem of my razor and fresh clothes being locked up with a simmering Pam. Somewhat to my surprise she came into the pilothouse full of contrition, apologizing for her outburst and inviting me back to the stateroom to get washed and dressed. The change of heart was, I thought, awfully sudden–I expected several days and a lot of fast-talking would be needed, and even that might not have worked. I decided not to look too closely into her motives, just accept things for now.

The voyage to Balboa and the Panama Canal was indeed a pleasant yachting trip. The weather was fine, the Mela made light work of the swells, several people got all-over sun tans on the foredeck, and several had to be treated for over-exposure of delicate parts of the body which don't normally get that much sun. Mary and Leah proved capable ship's cooks, though I had reservations about how they were going to manage in the considerably more impressive waves of the Atlantic. The trip was a great success so far.

Pam devoted considerable effort to trying to get me to tell her why we were going to the Mediterranean, but I put her off with the assurance that I would hold a briefing for everyone when we were safely out in the Atlantic.

"One of the passengers we are picking up there is the real expert on what we're doing." I explained, "so it will be less confusing to have her to get the details right." With that she had to be content, but it didn't stop her trying. Rather enjoyable really.

I had a talk with Joe about improving the Finder for the job we were going to. I wanted zoom capability to look at seafloor details. Joe thought about it.

"The system can't see anything smaller than a couple of centimeters anyway, and not that at great depth because of the losses in transmission. Still, I can probably do something for shallow water. How deep are we working?"

"We really need a thousand meters, call it three thousand feet, more for a survey."

"You want me to work while everybody else is lazing about enjoying themselves?"

"Now Joe, you like working, and you certainly don't need a sun tan."

He chuckled. "I'll see what I can do, but I don't think you can expect much detail in deep water."

He spent considerable time in his house on the aft deck, appearing occasionally in a trance as usual when he was engrossed in something new. Judith resumed her station as his keeper for the duration. He announced just before we got to Balboa that we could zoom in on the bottom, but until we tried it he didn't know how much detail we would get. I promised to stop for a while in the lakes to let him test it before we got out in the Atlantic.

Mikel and Natasha were waiting for us with a load of camera gear to store, as was our credit for fuel and stores. They have a pleasant Czech accent that I thought added a nice cosmopolitan touch to our ill-assorted crew. I gave them a private briefing on the situation, and introduced them to the rest of our crew. Things were pumped and carried onto the Mela until she was noticeably lower in the water, now I hoped capable of making the Canaries with enough left to go on to the Mediterranean if we had to. The yacht club entertained us royally, and we took some strolls to stretch our legs in preparation for a long time shut up in the boat. Pam was never allowed alone long enough to get to a telephone, so even if our suspicions were well founded she couldn't do any harm. We thought.

Very interesting going through the Canal. Everyone had right of way over us so we had plenty of time to test the Finder. When he was ready Joe called me to his laboratory, if I may call it that, and I brought Mikel and Natasha for their first exposure to it. Their reaction was the usual one when Joe turned on the old view, which showed a section of the water round us as if we were looking into it at an angle, including trying to put their hands in it. Then Joe switched to the new computer program. We were now looking into the box as if we were looking down on the bottom from a few feet up. Every rock and pebble on the bottom in beautiful green detail. Mikel said something that sounded like a Czech swearword. Natasha tried to touch it again.

"Oh, oh," she said, "we can find things nobody has seen for thousands of years, do a complete inventory on the best places."

"You're the expert Natasha," I told her, "you can pick where we go. It'll take us weeks to get there, so you can plan the survey."

"Can I get on the Internet from the boat?"

"Yes, but no chat rooms or anything, read only–we're trying to keep all this to ourselves until you publish it with pictures."

Mikel in the mean while had been taking photos of the box. As far as we could tell on the little screen on his camera the discs would show everything to be seen without 3-D, so he was happy. I didn't have a reader for the odd discs his camera used, so couldn't show them on the pilothouse computer. Mikel was impressed, but Natasha the trained archeologist was beside herself with impatience to get the Finder to work on something real.

"The invention of the century, this is going to revolutionize underwater archeology." She was repeating what others had said before her, 'invention of the century.' Joe was positively purring. The rest of us had more or less got used to it, so he reveled in the admiration of someone new. I must say the downward zoom was a revelation to me too, I could barely restrain myself from trying to touch it.

At dusk we dropped our required Panamanian chaperone and headed out into the Atlantic. I called up the program to start the computer steering us on the great circle route to the Canary Islands, then Mike and Blake and I went carefully through the whole boat. I wanted to be certain everything was secure, so nobody would get brained by a flying can of carrots or crushed by an avalanche of potatoes if we got into rough weather.

That first night out with plenty of fresh food to choose from Leah and Mary produced a splendid prime rib dinner, in two sittings, as there wasn't room for ten round the table. I sat in on the second, with the cooks and Natasha for company. Natasha was very impressed with the accommodations on this boat.

"Last expedition boat we were on, had one bathroom for boat. Now we have one all for ourselves."

Leah and Mary were fascinated.

"You mean men came in to pee while you were in there?"

"One bathroom for boat, everybody in together."

They were obviously bursting to cross-examine Natasha for details when they could get her alone.

After dinner I gathered everyone in the salon for the promised briefing.

"Some of you are wondering why we are going to the Mediterranean, and why we left without telling anyone where we were going."

Pam muttered something I didn't catch that seemed to have a lot of 's' sounds in it. I ignored her and continued.

"Joe's old company, SQV Corporation, is trying to steal Joe's invention, and they've got the FBI helping them. Our plan is to make some significant discoveries in the Mediterranean, well out of their reach, and get them published to show in public that it's ours and what a great thing Joe has done. Mikel and Natasha are with us to write the article for Geographica. Natasha is an expert on ancient wrecks, so she's planning a survey in deeper water off the places where shallow water wrecks have been excavated. With Joe's new zoom system most of them can probably be dated just from the Finder pictures. What we're hoping for is some really old stuff, to make a dramatic debut for the Finder. Now I've told you more than I know on the subject, so Natasha can answer questions."

There were plenty, mostly on what old wrecks looked like. People were a bit disappointed to hear they were usually just a pile of amphora, as some of us had visualized six thousand-year-old boats with ragged sails waving in the current and skeletal crews still on deck.

"But," Natasha explained, "it's the amphora that matter. Every place and time had their own special shape, we know a lot about a ship just from this."

Some people wanted to know about finding treasure, but Natasha disabused them of that notion. "All belongs to country where found, goes to national museums when study finished. Anyway, we look too deep to get anything to surface even if we found any. Archeological treasure, that's what we find."

And with this they had to be satisfied.

It was an idyllic voyage, a real yachting trip. The weather was warm and mild, the machinery worked flawlessly, Leah and

Mary worked on making us all plump, suntans were completed down to the most intimate corners. However, a seventy foot boat isn't very big for ten people and there was some snapishment and groundless spats by the time a couple of weeks had passed. We'd all seen all the DVDs, even the ones Blake brought, so time began to pass slowly. Otherwise things were going very well. The old boat leaked only the few drops to be expected of a wooden hull and I found we were using much less diesel than I expected.

The only worrying factor was that I couldn't get through to William on the satellite phone. His number rang, but he seemed to have left the answering machine off. I wanted to know what happened when the recording of the FBI racial insults to Joe became public. Well, William was probably busy, in court perhaps, so I decided to try again in a few days.

After dinner a few days before we were due to reach the Canaries I made an announcement. "We've got so much fuel left, and the food is holding out so well, that I've decided to go straight on to Gibraltar or maybe Marseilles, and skip the stopover."

A concerted animal snarl arose from my loyal crew and erstwhile friends. I found myself in the position of a lion tamer who discovers too late that he has left his whip and chair in the dressing room. I suddenly decided we would stop off for a break at Santa Cruz, Tenerife, and so informed them just in the nick of time. I must say the Internet site for the Canaries made it sound irresistible –

"This paradisiac group of islands, with a preferred climate and constant temperature through all the year . . ."

I thought myself the place was rather touristy and crowded, but my crew vanished into it like gophers into their burrow. It took me three days to get them all back, loaded with junk souvenirs. Everybody was happy and temperaments were much improved by the run ashore. I now had two worries. The nagging concern that I couldn't reach William, and that I wasn't certain in the confusion that Pam had not got to a telephone while we were in harbor.

Chapter 6

Mary and Leah shopped for fresh food but I didn't care for the price of diesel oil in the Canaries. We still had plenty, so I decided to push on to Marseilles where the price was better and I could get a Cat mechanic to come and give the engine a look over, change all the filters, clean the injectors, in fact spruce the engine room up generally. I had fitted a power oil changer to keep the engine clean, but apart from that it had now run some seven weeks continuous without service.

I was really worried about William. I had tried several time to call him with no answer. Once we were at sea bound for the Straits of Gibraltar I settled down in the middle of the night local time to find someone in California to help. I reached Jerry, my yacht broker and long time friend.

"Jerry, can you check on William for me? His number doesn't answer, and doesn't take a message. If you can spare a moment, maybe you can see if he's home."

Jerry was semi-retired, I knew he had plenty of time to look for William and contacts all over town. Two hours later he called back.

"Sorry, got bad news for you." My heart sank. "I located William. He's in Torrance Memorial. Somebody broke into his condo and beat him up and ransacked the place."

"How badly is he hurt? Has there been anything in the newspapers or on TV about us?"

"I'm going to see him. The hospital says 'improving' but I don't know improving from what. Why should there be anything in the news about you? What have you done now?"

"Nothing. Call me back as soon as you get to him. Call me on your cell phone, perhaps he can talk too."

He promised to drive to the hospital as fast as he could. So, they had got to William and he hadn't been able to send the recording out. That was a definite problem, apart from the concern that William had been hurt badly enough to have been in hospital for at least several days. We had the original recording of course. In my private safe deposit box in Santa Monica.

Jerry called back from William's room. He claimed to be fine, just being kept for observation in case of internal injuries.

"William," I told him, "you're not fooling us. You must have been hurt pretty bad. Sorry, we never thought of the FBI getting violent. Did you see who did it?"

"No, but it wasn't FBI, these guys were too short. They took the discs though, I couldn't send them."

"Don't worry about it, we'll manage. Get well and look after yourself. Call us once in a while, you know my satellite number."

"Sorry, I don't remember it. Can't seem to remember some things. You call me. Call in the night when it's lonely here."

That didn't sound good. "When do you think you'll be going home?" I asked.

"Soon. Pretty soon."

"Are you OK for the hospital bills? Anything you need?"

"No problem, but I'm going to charge this to Mela as a business expense later."

"That's fair. Here, the rest of the firm wants to talk to you. If we're not tiring you."

We promised to call him every day. When the phoning was over the firm held a board meeting. The problem to discuss was that I was the only one who could get to the safe deposit box, it took my signature in person. Even if this was a good moment to fly back to California there was an element of risk in it. Not only that I didn't want to join William in Torrance Memorial, we couldn't afford to risk losing the original record. We reluctantly gave up on the propaganda campaign, as there didn't seem to be anything practical we could do.

On our way to Marseilles Natasha gave us her suggestion for the most effective survey article she could produce.

"I think we should concentrate on a specific area, not try and cover the whole Mediterranean. It would be winter before we finished, and you won't want to be touring the Mediterranean when the Mistral is on."

No argument with that.

"I think we should tour round Crete at about the thousand meter line. There should be hundreds of ancient wrecks there, and we have the only equipment to see them at that depth."

Joe had been working with her. "We'll cruise slowly along places flat enough for wrecks to accumulate, watching a wide angle view. Then when we come to a likely place we'll have to stop so the water flowing past doesn't make so much noise. Otherwise there won't be any detail on the narrow beam mode. It'll be slow, but the charts show the bottom's too steep for wrecks to stay on it in a lot of places."

This sounded like a good plan to the rest of us non-experts, and was adopted with acclaim.

Marseilles is a busy commercial port, full of cranes working, real tugs bustling about, bright lights at night, things being hoisted, dropped, and sworn at. Humming with the noise of trucks moving containers and ship's sirens announcing they were leaving, turning, backing, or ready to fight for position. Overwhelming for us who were used to the quiet of the open sea and the drowsy beat of the diesel. We got a mechanic to spend a day on the machinery at vast expense. While we were refueling an interesting incident occurred. Leah was out on deck watching two scruffy dockworkers handling the hoses. One made a remark to the other about the American girl, in which I caught the word 'vache.' French has to be spoken slowly and distinctly for me to follow it, so I don't know what else he said. Leah looked up and out of her mouth came a stream of gutter French in which I caught about one word in ten. The monologue finished, if I heard correctly, with the opinion that the subject, standing with his mouth hanging open, owed his presence to his mother's career as a businesswoman among the tents of the Foreign Legion.

"Formidable!" He said, and concentrated on the fueling hose.

"Leah," I asked, "where did a nice girl like you learn to speak French like that?"

She grinned. "Father was in the service, we were stationed in France for years. We played with the local children, learned all the good words."

"Yes, you certainly did. I think that may come in useful one day." The faint stirring of an idea had come to me, a backup plan if anything else went wrong.

As soon as the Mela was full of fuel and supplies we set off past Sardinia and Sicily heading for Crete. A week of avoiding the busy traffic of the Mediterranean brought us to the thousand-meter line, ready to start the business that we had now spent so much time and money on.

I won't describe everything we found, most of it boring in the extreme. We traveled a thousand miles circumnavigating Crete, which isn't a very big island. Some places had nothing, some on the south side had so many wrecks we didn't know how we'd store all the data. The wrecks I recognized, big motor and steam ships, warships from at least two wars, fishing boats innumerable, Natasha ignored except when they were lying on her sort of wrecks. Her wrecks, stored on carefully filed removable hard discs of vast capacity, photographed by Mikel, and carefully keyed to GPS positions, were mostly just barely ship-shaped piles of weed-grown junk. The crew quickly tired of watching our slow progress, but Natasha was in ecstasies over what we were finding.

"Today we find Phoenician I think, maybe an Egyptian but I can't tell. Treasures, treasures. We'll be famous." Most evenings at dinner Natasha was bubbling over with the wonders of the day, but I'm afraid the rest of us surfeited with piles of rock and litters of amphorae quite early in the three solid weeks the survey took us, working night and day.

The work may have been dull, but I can tell you it kept me as captain and Mike and Blake as mates desperately busy. We following our erratic and apparently illogical course through fleets of fishing boats, across busy trade routes, almost through several sailing yachts, and over and around innumerable hazards to our little ship. Right in the middle of some tricky avoidance of highly indignant local boats the intercom frequently added to our troubles by insisting we reverse course and slow down because there was something interesting on the sea floor right under an approaching freighter. Leah and Mary did their best, but the situation often got too complicated for them so one of us with more experience had to be on hand all the time. The rules of the road are complicated enough when you've passed an examination on them, which I had, and when everyone follows them, which one couldn't rely on. Mary and Leah eventually concluded that everyone piloting a ship in the Mediterranean was completely crazy, a view which is not entirely inaccurate. Our behavior was, one has to admit, even crazier than the locals, as they couldn't imagine what we were doing. I was constantly afraid we were going to get somebody's navy out to find out, but the Turks and Greeks were too busy with their own feud and joint running battle with the UN to bother about us.

When we finally arrived back at the exact position we had started the survey from, just in time to save some of our sanity, Natasha hopefully requested we go back and do some of it over at a different depth. The only repeatable reply to this out of the unanimous chorus of unworkable suggestions as to what she could do with her wrecks was a female voice which, in penetrating tones, made it clear that the only way Natasha was going to revisit this coast was by swimming.

"Now, now," I told them, "Natasha is doing her best to get us a really memorable write-up. I do think though we've got enough material for a dozen articles already, so we'll head back to Marseilles to resupply while Natasha writes her piece for Geographica. It is a pity we can't download the photos to the ship's computer, because then we could send the whole article by email and save a lot of time."

"Why can't we?" This from Joe in a peevish tone of voice.

"Because the funny discs the camera uses don't fit any of the holes in the computer." I explained.

"Hasn't the" – some word I didn't quite catch – "camera got an interface cable?"

Mikel answered. "Yes, but there's no socket on the computer to plug it into."

"Helpless bunch of bastards, it should be simple enough. You should have told me before. Tomorrow, when I've had some sleep, I'll look at it."

As I said, everyone had been under a lot of strain, and Joe had been in the laboratory most of the last three weeks. Judith took him away for a quiet time and some rest.

We followed the normal traffic pattern back toward Marseilles, which made the piloting much easier and safer. The multi-lingual chorus of conflicting and usually incomprehensible remarks addressed to us by indignant captains was stilled. Natasha and Mikel worked most of the nights and days on selecting the photos to use and writing the article round them. When Joe was rested he started work on the camera problem.

"See," I told him, "there aren't any holes to plug the cable into."

"Stand back, whitey, and let a real man at it."

"If you get uppity Joe you'll have to go to the back of the boat."

"My hut's already at the back of the boat."

Natasha looked from one to the other of us with her mouth hanging open, expecting violence to break out. After a moment she realized we were both laughing. "You two good friends, yes?" She said doubtfully.

"I count it a privilege to be a friend of Joe's," I told her.

While we were talking Joe had released some secret spring and the computer had popped out of the dash so that its rear was visible. It sprouted several cables that vanished into the dark space beneath, and had a whole row of empty sockets to match the camera cable. Joe plugged the cable into one of them and threaded it through so it emerged from the top drawer. He dropped the computer back into its nest.

"Right, now plug the camera in."

Nothing happened. The clouds that the computer played with on the screen when it was bored continued to drift by. "Reboot it." Joe commanded.

This produced a result of sorts. A mystery message appeared on the screen.

"Nikoso.exe not found"

"Where's the disc the camera came with?" Joe asked Mikel.

"In my desk drawer at home." Was the gloomy reply.
"I think I need a drink," said Joe.

Chapter 7

I looked at Mikel. He slunk off to bring Joe a glass of our rapidly shrinking stock of Chivas. Joe took it, opened the pilothouse door, and went to sit on the bench below the pilothouse windows. The roll of the boat banged the door shut and silence fell. When Mikel could no longer stand the atmosphere of mute accusation he spoke, avoiding Natasha's eye.

"Well, how was I to know we'd need it?"

Natasha answered in a rapid incomprehensible hiss. I can't tell you what she said, because it was in what I presume to be Czech. Mikel wandered off below followed by Natasha still talking. I laid down on the watch bunk to relax for a moment. The gentle roll and the purr of the diesel were too much for me. I woke with a start concerned that nobody was minding the boat in one of the busiest waterways in the world. A scan round the horizon and check of the radar reassured me that none of the traffic was on a constant bearing, so I had not slept us into an emergency.

The click of the keyboard had woken me. Joe was typing rapidly, wandering the World Wide Web via the satellite phone plugged into its socket by the computer screen. He picked up Mikel's camera while he copied something off the back into the computer. After a pause he sat on the helm seat and grinned at me.

"Just wait 'till you get your phone bill. The camera program's downloading at three kilobytes. It said 'estimated time 8 hours' when it started, but I don't think it'll take quite that long."

"Joe, by now that's a drop in the bucket. All we can do is go all out to succeed. If we fail we'll be in hiding anyway, so the bills won't matter."

It didn't take eight hours, it took three-quarters of an hour. Even so, at satellite rates the bill was going to be memorable. When the program was safely installed Joe turned on the camera and started calling up the pictures in its current memory. They came up rather slowly but very crisp and clear. Joe clicked the mouse a couple of times and peered at the result.

"Hmm," he said, "Mikel has done all these in high definition. A bit wasteful, they won't reproduce any better. Still, perhaps that's what magazines want. They're going to take a long time to send, make the Phone Company rich."

"Mind the boat, I'm going to fetch Natasha back to show her it's OK now."

I found the Geographica team still hissing at each other in the salon. Natasha gave a squeak of joy when she saw the screen. She and the provisionally forgiven Mikel settled down to edit photos, leaving very little room to pilot the boat.

It took them the daylight hours of two days to finish the article, safely stored in HTML with JPG pictures. That's OK, I don't know what it means either, but they were happy with it.

"Ready, we send to Judy now," announced Natasha.

"Not right now," I reminded her, "it's the middle of the night. Call her when it's morning there so she's ready to receive it."

The authors, Joe, and I gathered quietly at one in the next morning full of excited anticipation. I keyed the US access number and handed the phone to Mikel.

"Just the area code and local number," I told him.

He dialed, then hit three more numbers for the extension. There was a long pause.

"Hello?" Who's this?" he said.

We couldn't hear the reply, but Mikel looked alarmed. "But where's Judy?"

"What . . . when? Put me over to the boss."

A pause then "It's Mikel. What happened? What about our article?"

"No, no impossible, I call again."

He switched off the phone with a stunned expression.

"It is impossible. I do not believe."

"What, what?"

"Judy disappeared a week ago. The police think she was kidnapped. The editor in chief never heard of our article, said the magazine's set for the next twelve issues. He says come home, we go on another assignment while he looks at our stuff to see if he wants to publish it after."

I hated to see a grown man cry, particularly when it's me. I stared out into the black night and wondered if drowning was such a bad way to go. Tears were rolling down Natasha's cheeks and Mikel was swearing softly in Czech. Joe rested his head on the dash and I think he was crying. Ten minutes of contemplating the black windows restored some life to my stunned brain.

"OK, now we pull ourselves together," I told them firmly, "we're not beaten yet. You two, do you want to go back to Geographica or will you go with us?"

Joe interrupted. "What can we do now? We're beaten, every way we try they've already closed off. Now they've killed that poor woman. These two will be out of a job after all that work. Let's give up while we've still got some money left."

"No!" Natasha dried her eyes on Mikel's sleeve. "We go on. The hell with Geographica, their loss. We think of something. You," looking at me, "you tell us what to do next."

I turned the satellite phone on to call William. He was home, though still not very well.

"William," I told him, "we're in big trouble. I'll tell you the details later, right now act lawyer for us. Look up the present law on exporting strategic data. I know it's changed a lot, are there any restrictions left? We need to know as soon as you can. Call me right back."

"Tell us," Joe commanded.

I sketched out my plan, and they were suitably impressed.

"Never, you'll never work that." Mikel, still in pessimistic mood.

"You're out of your mind." My friend Joe.

"Do it, we win, you can do it." Natasha full of quite unjustified faith in her captain.

The phone beeped and I picked it up. William had been quick, had looked it up in the virtual law library on the Web.

"Ready? This is the list of things you need an export license for. I'll go through each item, check those you're planning to contravene."

"Go ahead," I replied, "I'll check any I don't understand with Joe."

"Weapons and explosives."

"No"

"Certain cryogenic sensors."

I repeated this unlikely item to Joe. "Infra red surveillance, nothing to do with us."

"No," I told William.

"Machined steel tubing."

Joe explained. "Gun barrels."

"No."

"Bipropellant reaction propulsion devices."

"No."

"Fissionable materials other than medical devices."

"No."

"That's the list."

"What about computers and encryption devices?"

"Not on the list any more, the controls have been relaxed a lot in the last few years."

"So the Serpent Finder is uncontrolled?"

"As far as I can see yes. I'm not a specialist in this sort of law, but it seems clear enough. What are you up to now?"

I explained the mess we were in and my plan to recover the situation. He joined the majority side. "You must be crazy, they'll never go for that!"

"You got any better idea?"

"No, but that doesn't mean there isn't one. I'll think about it."

I switched the phone off and briefed the others. "No problem, we're free to do anything we like with the Finder."

"What does William think of your scheme?"

I thought it best not to discourage them any more than they already were. "He's thinking about it, but he says there's nothing illegal about it."

Leah appeared in a see-through robe to take the next watch.

"Just the person I want to talk to," I told her, trying not to look down, "I have a little job for you. First, look on the Web for Terreau CSF, try to find the name of a top man there. You are

54

going to be the secretary to the president of the Mela Corporation and you're going to get him on the phone for me. Tomorrow I'll tell you what to say."

"What does a secretary to the president get paid?"

A reasonable question. "If we pull this off, it pays something nice in diamonds. If we don't, none of us get anything. Now we're all going to bed. Are you OK by yourself on watch or do you need a lookout?"

"I'll get Mary. We'll call you if there's any trouble."

We trooped off to our respective cabins. I don't know how much sleep the others got – I was awake a long time planning how to approach Terreau. Perhaps I should explain that they are a very big French electronics company, a major producer of electronic warfare devices and suchlike. With lots of money.

In the morning I held a meeting of the board of directors of the Mela Corporation. Mike, Blake, Joe, and I gathered on the foredeck in the pleasant breeze of the Mela's steady eight knots so I could bring them all up to date and get their approval of our new plan. Joe had already expressed his opinion. The other two were unanimous.

"You're out of your mind!"

"Go on," I told them, "tell me what's wrong with it."

"For a start," Mike raised his voice more than necessary, "they'll never go for it. It's a waste of effort."

"In that case, I've wasted some effort, but that's all. We haven't committed to anything or spent any money on it, where's the harm in trying?"

"Because it's illegal, you can't do that."

"I spoke to William. He looked it up in the Internet law library. It's perfectly legal. Any other problems?"

Mike spoke suddenly. "Why?"

"Why what?"

"Why was Judy removed a week ago? Why then?"

At first I thought it a silly question. Then it slowly dawned on me what he meant. I pulled out the satellite phone to call the Phone Company.

"Hello? Can you give me the numbers this phone called from two weeks ago to a week ago?"

She could. All but one I recognized. I put that stranger in the phone's memory, pressed the auto dial, got an immediate answer. A computer spoke.

"This is the SQV Corporation. If you know the extension number you want dial it now, otherwise stay on the line and an operator will assist you."

"We have not," I told the assembly, "been as careful about security as we should have. Someone called SQV from this phone eight days ago, just when someone could see the survey succeeding."

"Pam?"

"No way to tell, Pam seems the most likely, but it could have been anybody. We all have a big stake in the project's success, but none of the girls do. From now on, everything is secret, tell the girls as little as possible. Meetings like this somewhere private. I'll start locking the phone up when it's not in my pocket. Especially at night. All we can do now is go ahead – what about my scheme?"

Mike cross-examined. "What are you going to do with all that money if you do get it? We couldn't spend that much in our whole lives. Be fun trying though."

I told them what I had in mind. Blake went off in the silence to fetch a bottle and some glasses. When everyone was lubricated I spoke again.

"Well, what about it? Do I go ahead?"

The verdict of the board of directors was unanimous, delivered by Mike, William unavoidably absent.

"This'll be the craziest thing we've ever thought of, including the Alaska trip. Let's do it. Here's to Federal prison."

"Then not a word about it to anyone, not the girls, not even each other. Forget it, put it out of your minds until we're ready. One premature word and I don't know what will happen. Remember, William is still recovering from being almost beaten to death, Judy may very well be dead, we are taking on people who can call for helicopter gunship backup."

That called for more Chivas. A very solemn board meeting adjourned to think about it. I intercepted Joe to get a resume from him. "One page, but put the good stuff in, like what you did at MIT."

Mary and Leah had spent their watch on the Web learning everything they could about Terreau. The telephone bill was approaching my rapidly falling net worth. They had a list of people I might want to talk to, but as they didn't know what I wanted to say they left it to me to pick one. I selected a Monsieur Lemaire as the right contact.

"Now, Leah. You're the President's secretary. Get hold of M. Lemaire's secretary and make a friend out of her. Exchange stories about your bosses, chat, get his email address if you can. Then ask for him to talk to me. If she wants to know what about, say your boss only told you 'a matter of mutual profit.' If he insists, it concerns a valuable cross-licensing agreement. Can you do that?"

"Well, depends what sort of secretary he's got. If she's all business and won't chat, what do I do?"

"Try and get him to talk to me anyway. Sound very businesslike too."

We waited until ten o'clock, plenty of time for M. Lemaire to get settled in his office. Leah worked her way through a succession of organizational levels until she said "Bingo" followed by a conversation in French much too fast for me to follow. Part way through she giggled and whispered an aside with her hand over the mouthpiece.

"She wants to know if I'm your mistress too or just your secretary. I said unfortunately you had a charming mistress and no time for me after work."

The conversation resumed. Eventually just before I burst with impatience she handed me the phone. "You have to get on first, then him. Is that OK?"

"This time it is," I said taking the phone.

Chapter 8

"Monsieur Lemaire?"
"Un moment sil vous plait."
"Oui?"
"Monsieur Lemaire, I wonder if it would be convenient to speak English? I regret my French is not as accomplished as your English."
"Tell me what you want, I am a very busy man."
"Mela Corporation owns an important new development in the field of underwater surveillance, suitable for your weapons division. It has also medical and industrial applications yet to be developed."
"I regret," he broke in to my dismay, "such an invention would have to come to us from a major corporation, someone we already deal with. I have innumerable approaches like this, rarely worth following up."
"Monsieur . . . "
"Je regret, non."
"I understand," I told him, "but perhaps I could trouble you to do one small thing, it may be to your advantage."
"Well?"
"Our chief engineer is Dr Joseph Jenkins. His MIT doctoral dissertation," here I read from Joe's resume, "*Coherent detection of multiple simultaneous signals* is, I am told, a classic in its field. If one of your technical advisors would look it up he might suggest a small further interest in your part."
"I will consider it."
He hung up without another word.
My board of directors expressed their unanimous opinion. "Told you so."
I checked the sea round us for emergencies before calling all-hands meeting to spread the bad news.
"I'm sorry, this trip is turning out worse and worse. I really don't know what to do next. It's going to be a long time before the Mela goes home, so here's everybody's chance to get out of

here on a nice airplane. I'll buy tickets to LAX for anyone who wants one."

"We stay," announced Natasha, "we not give up."

I'm not sure by his face that Mikel agreed. Leah and Mary spoke almost together.

"Let us think about it, talk it over."

"OK, all of you think about it and let me know before we get to Marseilles."

The phone beeped. I half expected what I heard.

"Un moment pour M. Lemaire."

"This is an unexpected pleasure monsieur," I told him with as much sincerity as possible.

"You will be amused by what my engineer said about Dr. Jenkins."

I very much doubted it. Angry perhaps. Terrified even. Amusement seemed a very unlikely emotion at that moment.

"Comment?"

"He said 'never mind the license, try and hire Jenkins for us.' I suppose that is impossible?"

"Not at all monsieur. If we could conclude a satisfactory cross licensing agreement you would in effect have Dr. Jenkins working for you. However, he is a major stockholder in the Mela Corporation so I doubt if he would leave us for a salaried position. He also owns the Mico Electronics Company outright, I think you would find him rather an independent worker."

"A pity. In the circumstances we are willing to examine the device you are offering us. When may we see it?"

"As soon as you can get to Marseilles, monsieur, it is on our research vessel which will reach the harbor tomorrow."

I had started to think of an appropriate way to tell the board 'I told you so' when Lemaire dashed my hopes again.

"Oh, non, non, that is quite impossible. We would have to see it in Paris where we have facilities."

"But Monsieur," I tried not to whine, "it weighs many hundreds of kilos, even if it were portable, what would your esteemed customs say to it?"

I couldn't shake his position. Paris or nothing.

"Very well, I'll put it to my board and see what they say. We've only contacted Terreau so far as the best partner, we may have to reconsider that."

"As you will. Call me when you have your equipment in Paris."

I put the telephone carefully back in my pocket. I could have stayed quietly at home, I had plenty of money, there were always pleasant girls about, Chivas Regal, fine restaurants. Instead a mutinous crew surrounded me, heading for a dirty noisy port from which I didn't know where to go next. I addressed them again.

"There's been a slight change of plans. We're going to Paris instead."

Mike had a question.

"Are we taking the Finder? How do we do that?"

"Easy," I told him with my usual show of totally unjustified confidence, "we drive the Mela Mermaid."

"You're a lunatic. How are you planning we do that? Put wheels on this wreck and drive it down the freeway?"

"There's a French canal system which will take us to Paris in about ten days, no problem."

Well, that proved a rather optimistic assessment.

"No!" announced Pam.

"What?"

"I came on this fucking boat for a week on the West Coast. I've been on it for months now, bored out of my skull, going places I didn't want to, nothing to do except worry, the same people, the same talk, the same food, now you say ten days in a fucking canal, it's never going to end, it's a fucking nightmare. I want to wake up, let me go home. I'm going to get a job and live like a normal person, I never want to see any of you again in my whole life. Blake and his crew of hookers can get along without me."

I felt as if I'd been kicked in the stomach. It took me a few moments to put my brain back together. I went on to get all the bad news.

"Joe?"

"I stay with the Finder."

"Blake?"

"I'm sorry, this isn't fun any more. I want to go home."

I took my key ring apart, handed some to Pam. "Blake, do me one last favor. See Pam gets to my beach house while she looks for a job and a place of her own. Pam, those are the keys to my pad and the Mercedes. Use them as long as you like."

They both nodded without saying anything.

"Judith?"

"I'll stay until we get to Paris then decide."

Joe looked as bereft as I felt.

"Mike?"

I didn't expect his reply. "I understand how the others feel, but I'll stay to see it through."

"Mary and Leah?"

"We're till thinking about it."

"Decide by tomorrow when I get the plane tickets."

I can't say the evening had much amusement and stimulating conversation. About like a particularly strict silent monastery I'd say. When I'd handed the watch to Mike I found Pam still awake. I had to find out why.

"I thought we had something good going, I didn't know you felt like that."

"No, you didn't. You've never grown up, that's your problem. You play nice with your doll when you're in the mood, than want to put me back in the box while you do something else. I'm not a doll, I'm a person. We're all people, this is real life. You get people beat up and killed and it's like you lost some play pieces. I think you need to see a shrink before you cause a real disaster."

I felt as if she'd stirred my brain with a spoon. Instead of going to bed I went up and sat on the foredeck with the stars to think things through. I wanted to say she had it wrong, I wasn't like that, but I couldn't. She understood me perfectly. I did think of her as a doll. And the other women too now I had to face myself. This whole trip, the whole idea, it's as loony as they've been telling me. What was I thinking of? How could I stop?

The pilothouse door opened for another orphan to join me. I judged by the size that Joe had come out for the same reason as mine. We sat in silence for a long time. I spoke first.

"I'm sorry Joe, I didn't know what I was doing. Let's give up, go live in Canada for a while, or travel, Australia, I've never been there. We can dump the Finder in the sea, sell the Mela, quit before I cause any more grief."

"Pam gave you a lecture?"

"Yes. Judith?"

"Yes."

After another long pause I went on. "They're both right, we're a couple of loonies. Alcoholic loonies, too."

"I'll go get a bottle and a couple of glasses, shall I?"

"Yes."

Even Chivas Regal only made us sadder. I started to speculate on the possible discomforts of drowning. I asked Joe how he thought it would be.

"You can swim, you'd struggle for hours, very uncomfortable. Don't do it."

Two or three drinks later Joe suddenly burst out "I'm damned if I will."

"Will what?" I asked, still thinking about drowning.

"The Finder is a real invention, the best thing I've ever done. I'll be fucked if I'll give up now."

"Goo ole Joe," I said just before I fell asleep on the hard locker cover.

An anxious search party wakened us, afraid we had jumped overboard in the night. We couldn't be seen from the pilothouse windows because we were sitting below them. Our respective cabins were now empty of hostile females so we retired to sleep the hangover off.

The shore party had its bags packed ready to leave before we even got tied up. Blake escorted Pam off the boat to customs on their way to the airport. I waved but neither of them turned back, just walked off out of my life leaving a very large hole. I cornered Mary and Leah.

"You two are sure you want to go on with this loony trip? You can leave now, no hard feelings, Mike and I understand."

"We'd like to see Paris again, you need secretaries to translate for you. Mike's sweet, Natasha is fun because she knows so much. But if we're going to work for Mela we want to get paid, no fun in Paris if we don't have spending money."

I hugged them both. "Thank you, thank you. I'll do my best to see you have fun in Paris. Now you can help me with the next problem. We need customs clearance, which may be a little sticky."

I had underestimated the effect of two well-built females speaking fluent French on the douanes. Their implication that M. Lemaire dictated the trip to Paris helped too. As did Leah's carefully calculated angle of lean over the official in charge's desk, revealing that her impressive contours were untrammeled by any underwear. After which, believe it or not, I had to take an examination to prove I could pilot my boat.

Armed with well-stamped papers we fuelled and provisioned for a drive through the French countryside. This turned out to be a rather high stress operation. The Mela suddenly became very large, awkward, hard to control, even willful, in the narrow turbulent stream full of unsympathetic bargemen in berets. No relaxed running on computer controlled autopilot here. Sweaty concentration at the wheel every second, that's what it took. Mikel tried it once, said he'd rather leave it to experts. Mary and Leah were rather good at it, including leaning out of the windows exchanging pleasantries with other traffic. Natasha also could hold her own after some learning experiences, fortunately damaging only pride and some paint. We ran only in daylight, turn and turn so nobody steered for more than and hour at a time. Those not steering kept a real lookout, behind as well as in front. Nobody complained about being bored.

Very empty, my cabin. The scent of Pam made it worse. The third night tied to a pier out of the traffic brought a visitor. Leah tapped on the door.

"I'm lonely by myself in that cabin, can I come and sleep with you?"

Before I had time to frame a polite refusal, she went on "just sleep, just for company."

"I'm lonely too, you're welcome. Only thing is, do you have, do you think you could . . . " She stared at me obviously framing a polite refusal, "Have you got a thicker nightgown?" The one she had on did not suggest 'just sleeping.'

"Oh, yes, certainly."

She reappeared in something in nice opaque flannel. Much more sisterly. I slept better that night than I had since Pam left.

Chapter 9

That endless drive through the canals into the Seine took even longer than I expected. I had nightmares about it for months afterward in which I steered immense amorphous ships backward down narrow streets in tiny rivulets of water among busy scenes of women pushing baby carriages and storefronts full of valuable antiques.

We got rather a pleasant mooring, tied up below a pedestrian walk in downtown Paris. This good fortune stemmed partly from the disbursement of significant amounts of euros but more to judicious deep breathing by Mary and Leah.

I learned from overhearing their innocent girlish chatter that Mary and Leah found the male reaction to their empenage highly amusing. Their unflattering discussions of the male intelligence led them to conclude that what little useful there might be in us lay in organs far removed from the brain. They had a private game, which I have an uneasy feeling may be universal to their sex. I'll explain for the education of any men who might have unwittingly awarded points in it. A point is scored if the player can produce an obvious physical male reaction in public without actually touching the subject. Mary and Leah had a house rule that the now absent Blake did not count, on the same grounds that sportsmen don't shoot sitting birds. My pretence not to have heard any of this precluded my asking how many points I had contributed, even if I really wanted to know.

We sat in the salon admiring the Paris scene, recovering from the final stress of tying up to a stone wall without scraping Joe's hydraphones off. Some of the party wanted to know what the something-or-other we were doing here. We had, you remember, decided to tell the girls as little as possible because we were certain that one of them spied for SQV. The way Pam had left seemed to eliminate her, though I had been sure she was the one. Judith particularly wanted to know what Terreau had to do with us.

"I can't tell you," I had to explain, "you haven't decided to stay with us. This is very private to the Mela Corporation. If you elect to be an outsider it's best you don't know."

I got a very odd look from Judith. Not the standard female 'turn brown at the edges and shrivel up, foolish man' look with which I had become only too familiar. Instead I thought her face showed a gleam of triumph. The expression came and went in a flash, but the impression stayed. Instead of the display of temperament I expected she took my refusal quite calmly.

"Yes, I can understand that. When I make up my mind I'll let you know."

When we were rested Leah resumed her position as secretary to the president. I didn't want anyone to hear our conversation with M. Lemaire so we took the phone for a walk along the embankment. Leah dialed her counterpart direct this time. She had another incomprehensible conversation with M. Lemaire's secretary, including another giggling aside to me, "I told her your mistress had left you so you're available. She hopes to meet you."

"Now Leah, let's not get carried away. I need to speak to Lemaire."

Some words I did understand were exchanged before I got the phone. "You have to be on first still," she whispered.

He started the conversation in his near-perfect English and usual affable easygoing manner.

"Well?"

"Bon jour M. Lemaire," I said in my best French, "Whenever it is convenient we are ready to demonstrate something that will impress you."

"First my chief engineer will visit you. If he thinks it worthwhile I may come. Tell my secretary where you are."

I handed the phone back to the president's secretary. "Arrange a meeting on the boat, tomorrow afternoon would be good."

Leah looked me straight in the eye with the phone behind her. "Please," she said.

I had done it again. "I'm truly sorry Leah, please would you arrange with his secretary for his chief engineer to visit us, preferably tomorrow afternoon."

"Better," she said.

M. Charpontier arrived on the embankment only half an hour late the next afternoon. Mary acted as corporate receptionist to escort him down the steps to the Mela Mermaid. I caught the quick sidelong glance between her and Leah which, I think, indicated Mary had taken unfair advantage to score an early point. We all had some difficulty taking him seriously at first because he looked exactly like Hercule Poirot in an old TV series infinitely repeated since the last century. A few minutes dispelled the wrong first impression. He seemed thrilled to meet Joe.

"Ah, Docteur Jenkins, this is an honor. I am familiar with your recent publications of course, but had not had the pleasure of studying your dissertation. Most illuminating. Your 'obviously' I learned to be wary of. It took me considerable thought to see how you reached some of your conclusions. Perhaps later you would be so kind to go perhaps for an apéritif so you may illuminate some of the points I had difficulty with."

Joe had a soulmate. "I'd be delighted Dr. Charpontier, after our business is concluded?"

"Ah, yes, business. What is it you wish to show me?"

By the direction of his eyes it wasn't the Finder he most wanted to see. I called him back to the matter in hand.

"This way," I told him, leading him through the salon past the door to Joe's lair.

Joe had arranged an interesting demonstration, with some of what he called 'image manipulation.' He started with a picture of a World War Two German fighter plane lying broken among some rocks with fish swimming in and out of it.

"Mon Dieu!" said our visitor, putting his hand in the box trying to touch the image.

The picture changed to a flat muddy surface swaying gently. M. Charpontier looked a question at Joe.

"That is a live image below the boat right now," Joe explained, "the gap which inconvenienced you coming aboard was to accommodate the transducer between the boat and the wall."

"Formidable!"

Next Joe played the disc of the nuclear submarine, with his new editing. We now appeared to drift over the sub as it passed beneath us so we saw both sides before it vanished out of the box. M. Charpontier's eyes were out on stalks.

"Encore," he requested.

He saw the submarine over and over after Joe assured him the picture time had not been altered. Then Joe showed it again in a peculiar jumpy slow motion.

"Ah," he exclaimed, "the pulse repetition rate, non?"

Joe smiled. "Have we shown you enough Monsieur? If you wish we can take a tour of the Seine to see live what's on the bottom."

"Non, non, je regret, I must return to my office at once, excuse me please." He rushed off with only a passing glance for the girls.

"I think," I informed Joe, "that your demonstration is a success."

"I'll drink to that," he answered, and we did.

I expected a call back from Lemaire that afternoon, but the phone remained silent. Tomorrow perhaps. At eleven I called William, figuring he should be out of bed by eight in the morning.

"How are you," I tried to ask casually, "are you well enough to travel?"

"You need someone to bail you out of prison?"

"No, but I think we are going to need some legal advice, contracts drawn up, a confidentiality agreement. Are you well enough to travel?"

"Where are you, tell me that before I agree to anything."

"Paris."

"I'm well enough to travel. I'm still using a crutch, so I'll come first class and you can pay the fare."

I could feel my credit card squirming again. "Give me an hour to make arrangements and the Mela Corporation secretary to the President'll call to say where to pick up the tickets."

"*Who?*"

"Leah."

"Oh. I think I need to come supervise what you guys are doing. You're sure you're not in jail?"

"Not yet, come and keep us honest. When can you leave?"

"It's eight now, could be at LAX by ten."

Leah started on airlines with my credit card in front of her. Half an hour later she called William.

"Here's what you do. You've got a passport? Good. Go to the Air France counter, they have a ticket for you on this morning's flight to get to Paris at nine tomorrow morning. No, don't be silly, it's a jet, remember the nine hour time difference."

Next morning I called an all-hands meeting. My crew was nervous and fidgety, remembering that my meetings were usually to share bad news.

"Today," I announced, "is a holiday for the Mela Corporation. Mike has my bankcard. He's going to a teller machine to get euros for everybody for spending money, some for Leah and Mary as an installment on their pay for sterling service to the corporation, and enough to take everybody to a real French lunch if they want. Don't hurry back, in fact nothing exciting is going to happen until we pick William up at the airport tomorrow morning."

Not one of my better predictions. The phone beeped. I had a presentiment who it might be so I handed the phone to Leah.

"Allo, Mela Corporation navire de recherches 'Mela Mermaid.' C'est de la part de qui?" A pause. "Oui, il est la. Ne quittez pas et je vous transferai."

She handed it back to me with a gesture of triumph. "M. Lemaire is on the line for you," she said, trying not to laugh.

"Good morning M. Lemaire. How are you this beautiful Paris day?" Don't overdo it, I warned myself.

"Somewhat fatigued, I sat in a senior management meeting very late last evening."

I'll just bet you did, I thought. Aloud I said "And what can I do for you?"

"We wish to have a larger party examine your device, if it is convenient. Two of our directors, some other technical people."

"When might this be?" I asked.

"Cette apres midi? I beg your pardon, you requested I speak English."

"N'importe. I understand, but there is a small obstacle. We have no confidentiality agreement between our companies, I think it would not be prudent to disclose Dr. Jenkins work too widely without some protection for both of us. Unfortunately our corporate attorney is at this moment waiting to board Air France's direct flight from Los Angeles, arriving tomorrow morning. I do not feel confident proceeding without his advice."

"Ah, yes. As you say, prudence. What do you suggest?"

"I think, M. Lemaire, we should hold a management discussion to develop some written agreement covering the eventualities both that you decide to negotiate for a licensing agreement, and the alternate that you decide against it."

"Un moment," I heard a whispered conversation at his end, "would it be possible for you to accommodate a visit by myself and one of our directors this afternoon? We are not capable of understanding the technicalities, mais the account given us by our chief engineer . . . "

"Oh, certainly," I told him. "As to the business meeting, let us leave it to our most capable secretaries to arrange." And so it was.

The crew were sitting drinking what they could hear of all this in. Leah switched the phone off to unleash a storm of questions. I waved for a chance to speak.

"There's been a slight change of plans." Groans all round. "No, no, nothing bad. Joe and I will have to stay on the boat to entertain a couple of visitors, M. Lemaire and a colleague. Sorry Joe. Everybody else go holiday right now."

If the boat had been on fire it couldn't have emptied faster. The two of us workers left behind sat in the salon to plan the demonstration. Joe had a complaint.

"You were a bit rash, weren't you?"

When Joe's annoyed with someone he tends to assume a trace of an Oxford accent, acquired when he studied some incomprehensible subject there on a scholarship.

"Why, what have I done?" I'd committed so many rash acts recently I couldn't think of one that stood out specially.

"We were going to keep the business with Terreau as quiet as possible, at least that we were thinking about licensing the Finder. You blurted it all out in front of everybody. I expect they'd all guessed most of it, but there's nothing secret now."

"Hmm. You're right Joe, I got so excited when Lemaire called me I forgot. Pam's gone, but I'm not so sure she was the spy. Well, nothing to do about it now. Anyway, it'll be public soon."

There wasn't anything I could do about it, so we concentrated on planning to impress this afternoon's visitors. A few minutes before they were due a sort of happy whirlwind shot into the salon, kissed me, said "Thank you, thank you," and disappeared below. Joe wanted to know what I'd done to deserve that, which I couldn't guess either. Presently Natasha reappeared with two rucksacks hanging off her.

"We go now, thank you, thank you, see you in a week, yes?"

She disappeared with a clatter, waving to us as she passed the cabin windows.

"I believe Mike has been very generous with your bank card," Joe remarked.

Chapter 10

M. Lemaire arrived on time, bringing an older man he treated with great respect, a director of the company by name M. Rousseau. I offered a choice of wines or spirits but they wanted to see the Finder first. Joe gave them the lot. Fish swimming, faint outlines of wrecks several thousand feet down, ancient piles of amphora, a bottle carefully placed under the Mela, and of course the celebrated nuclear submarine. Both of them tried to touch the images several times. Joe gave them a lecture on the possible development of industrial inspection devices based on the same technology, with the prospect for example of being able to look at flaws in the huge castings for the shafts of generators. He suggested medical possibilities, non-invasive imaging of fetuses and beating hearts, all calculated to raise the prospect of immense profits in their minds. When we thought they'd had enough I escorted them back to the salon and poured brandy all round. M. Lemaire had a try at getting us to discuss a deal, but I wouldn't play.

"Tomorrow, when our attorney is here to help us, we'll be happy to come to Terreau to see if we have a mutual interest." With that they had to be satisfied.

Joe and I went early to our lonely beds after a frugal supper. I woke hours later from a sound sleep to a muffled crash above, followed by peals of merry laughter. A little later came the unmistakable sound of two people with a lot of packages falling down the companionway to the cabin level. I prepared to leap out of bed to render first aid when the fallers burst into laughter again. I concluded they were either not hurt, or at any rate not feeling any pain. Several others then fell down the companionway in succession. The noises, some of which were very difficult to account for, gradually died away. Just as I dozed off again my cabin door burst open to reveal Leah, stark naked except for an elaborate hat with flowers, ribbons, and a veil, perched askew on top of her head. She pointed an accusing finger at me, said, "so that's where you've been hiding!" and sank slowly to the floor fast asleep. I wondered what the harvest had been if she had wandered through Paris in that outfit.

I lay for a while debating with myself the relative merits of leaving her where she was versus getting up and trying to put her back in her own cabin. I decided she probably wouldn't feel very well in the morning, so her own cabin would be better. I certainly didn't want her in my bed for several reasons, including the likelihood of an attack of acute nausea. I straightened her out as best I could so I could grasp her under the arms to half drag, half carry her to bed. I heaved her onto it and tried to take off the hat. Asleep as she was she strenuously resisted by putting both hands on top of it, so I left her as she was and went back to my own bed.

I reset my alarm an hour earlier because I'd planned on Mary or Leah guiding me to Orly Airport. I didn't expect either of them to be well enough, even if I could wake them in time.

The salon in the cold light of day was not a pretty sight. Torn wrapping paper littered everywhere, held down in places by empty wine bottles. Among the litter on the table I could see a gendarme's cap, half a chocolate cake, and a cage with a small parrot in it. The bird gave me a haughty look, said very clearly and distinctly "Bonjour, matelot" and turned its back on me. Joe and I had evidently missed a memorable day out.

I took coffee and croissants at a local café before taking a cab to Orly. The expense seemed to me insignificant compared with what Mike had done with my bankcard.

William came down the ramp last, escorted by two charming cabin attendants carrying his bags. He walked leaning heavily on a stick not, I was relieved to see, a crutch. He looked thinner than last time I'd seen him.

"William, you shouldn't have come if you're not well enough."

He grinned. "I'm well enough for first class on Air France with these charming ladies."

I brought him up to date on our latest escapades on the cab ride back to the Mela. Joe, sitting on the foredeck, waved us to come up. He hugged William, looked anxiously at him. You shouldn't have come if you're not up to it," he told him.

"That's what I said, but William has been making out with two French stewardesses all night so he says he's fine. Why are you sitting out here?"

"Because I'm not going to clear the mess up. The rest are all still asleep. They get ugly if you disturb them."

"I need one of them to translate in case the meeting goes French. I'm going to get Leah."

Leah answered my knock with "Go away, I want to die alone."

I bravely went in, turned on her shower. I left her on her feet in the shower swearing and denying she could even speak French. She emerged half an hour later, dressed, more or less in her right mind, pale and shaky. It occurred to me while we waited for her that somewhere in the computer was a file I might want for the meeting. Dragging a picture of a file to a picture of a disc is well within even my limited computer accomplishments. I opened a box of the old standard one inch 5 Meg discs, made two copies while I was about it. I stuck them in my shirt pocket and forgot them.

Lunch with a little white wine restored coherent speech to Leah. When she had settled she handed me a box. "We bought you a present yesterday, it's all ready to go." Considering it probably went on my bankcard I hoped I could afford it. Inside the box nestled a pocket communicator, a real full size one, not some fiddly thing in a watch or lapel pin. Universal, satellite and both cell phone standards. With a proper flip-up email screen.

"Thank you Leah, That's really thoughtful. Much better than my old sat phone."

Joe, William, and I plotted our tactics for the meeting over an excellent lunch.

"This is what I suggest," I told them. "We give them a license for sales to Europe, the Middle East, and Africa. We want a ten-percent royalty on all applications of Joe's technology, with an automatic license to use each other's new developments. We pay the same on sales in the US and Pacific Rim of new applications they develop. OK so far?"

They nodded.

"Then we want an advance payment against royalties to fund our development costs. It's using their money to do development for them, should be acceptable."

William frowned. "How much were you thinking of asking?"

"One million would be too small, they wouldn't take that seriously. I'll ask ten million, negotiate if I have to."

They both thought that was a lot of money but worth trying. Leah looked as if she wanted to disagree. "Go ahead, Leah," I encouraged her, "your opinion's worth hearing."

"Not enough."

Joe and William thought we should go with the ten, not risk spoiling the deal when we were so close. Leah expressed her opinion. "Cowards!"

Quite a large group met us outside the conference room. Out of the crowd came a cry of "Joseph!" followed by Joe's answering cry "Francois!" They met with hugs, shoulder punches, back slaps, tag ends of reminiscences. Obviously old friends. Francois explained.

"Joseph and I were together at Cambridge. I will never forget Joseph's thesis, 'Error correction limitations of N-dimensional convolution codes.' Most impressive."

On this happy if obscure note we drifted into the conference room. M. Rousseau chaired the meeting. After introductions the confidentiality agreement made up the first order of business. This involved arcane confusing discussions between William, his laptop, the Terreau attorney, his lap top, running in and out to print successive drafts, and bursts of translation by Leah. When the last detail had been satisfied M. Rousseau, William, their attorney, and myself all signed two copies. William put one carefully in his briefcase, nodded to me, signaling the real meeting to begin.

Joe then explained the principal of operation of the Finder, over all our heads on the front row but evidently comprehensible to the engineers and scientists in the second tier as it were. Then he gave a brief description of possible applications of the technology to other fields, including some that I couldn't see any connection to at all. But then I don't have a doctorate from MIT.

If that didn't soften them up for the deal we wanted I don't know what would. Francois acted as a cheering section throughout, which annoyed his management because they were carefully not showing too much enthusiasm. Then it came my turn to talk sordid details.

The general outline produced nods, no comments but no apparent resistance. Ten percent didn't raise an eyebrow. Then I came to the punchline, the up-front payment. I could hardly believe what I heard coming out of my mouth.

" . . . one hundred million dollars up front . . . "

I expected a show of indignation or a burst of laughter. I couldn't believe I'd said it. I finished my spiel, sat down, and waited for the storm. M. Rousseau spoke.

"Oui, bien, we will need to consider what you've said. Perhaps we could reconvene at this same time tomorrow? I think I need time to discuss the matter with the board."

We pried Joe out of a mass of engineers all talking at once. Once outside I got three simultaneous comments.

"Idiot."

"Lunatic."

"My hero!"

Encouraged by the minority opinion I put on a defense.

"Did they refuse? Did they? They didn't. They took time-out to think about it. That means a counter offer. I don't know why I said it, but the worst that can happen now is they offer the ten million we were ready to settle for to start with."

I have remarked before that I am a very poor prophet of the worst that can happen. Our taxi arrived at a mob scene with police cars flashing lights, fire engines flashing lights, and gendarmes rushing about giving the crowd orders everybody ignored. At the center of the excitement a milling crowd of French citizenry were all trying to look over the same spot on the embankment, the spot where we had left my boat. We pushed our way through the crowd, Joe's bulk helping spill Frenchmen right and left. The scene was nightmare come to life. The pilothouse roof had burned through revealing a gutted interior. Smoke had stained the outside of Joe's hut on the stern, hinting at more devastation within. Mike and Mary were sitting on the stone steps with their arms round each other, Mike's hands wrapped in bandages. Joe rushed down to them, brushing gendarme's clutching hands aside. William and Leah and I followed as best we could.

"Where's Judith, where is she?" Joe shouted.

Chapter 11

Mary looked miserably up at Joe. "Gone," she said.

"Gone? She's in there?" Joe pointed to the remains of the Mela Mermaid.

Mike answered. "Take it easy Joe, she's gone. We came up together to go to lunch before we tidied up. Judith went back for something, she said. She came back with a suitcase, ran past us across the road. There was a car waiting for her. I happened to look back at the boat, flames were coming out of the pilothouse. I went in, used the salon fire extinguisher on your laboratory. It's a mess but the fire hadn't gone far. While I was doing that the pilothouse really got going. The extinguisher ran out, I burned my hands on the pilothouse one. I'm sorry Joe."

I sat on the stone bench along the esplanade with my face in my hands. I must have talked aloud, my thoughts spilling out in public.

"It's hopeless. We can't win, I'm beaten. Send everybody home to try to put their lives back together. Poor Joe. Next somebody else is going to get killed. All our money'll be spent and nothing to show for it. Why didn't I stay home, I had a good life there. I'm going to live in the countryside, in France, on the money I have left. The hell with Terreau, SQV, the FBI. Just leave me alone."

I looked up to find the remains of my crew in a circle looking down at me. Joe stepped forward. "Go ahead," I told him, "hit me. It's all my fault."

The words he said didn't make sense at first, just ran round and round in my head like a cartoon caption on fast forward. When they settled I found he'd said, "We have not yet begun to fight."

"We've fought and lost, Joe."

"Oh no we haven't. We can rebuild the Finder, it was only a prototype anyway. If I ever catch that bitch I'll wring her neck, but she's gone, can't do any more harm. I don't know about your boat, but there are other boats. Maybe Terreau has a better one."

"What's Terreau going to say? What will they offer tomorrow?" I wallowed in my misery, which seemed to encourage the others. Leah chimed in.

"So you don't get a hundred million, they'll still want Joe's invention."

"A hundred million?" This in a duet by Mike and Mary.

Leah answered, "Our brave captain was supposed to ask for ten million as a down payment. He stood up there and asked Terreau for a hundred million down without stuttering or turning pale or anything."

I got two more divergent opinions.

"Crazy!"

"Let's go shopping again."

I took that as approval by Mary.

The gendarmes clamored for statements, apparently hoping one of us had done something they could arrest us for. Mary and Leah produced a fast stream of invective with gestures, which entertained the crowd no end. We promised to appear at the station to give statements 'later.' The two of them talked the chief gendarme into a promise to put a guard on the boat to discourage souvenir hunters instead.

The cabins below were almost undamaged. We got our clothes and personal stuff out, waved down a cab, and went to live in a hotel. Not too expensive, we specified. Leah settled down to look up boatyards in the telephone directory, to get the Mela out of the water for an expert assessment of the damage. The hotel didn't have Chivas Regal. We settled for brandy. Nobody felt like sleep, our nice separate rooms would be wasted tonight. About eleven something in my pocket beeped. I couldn't think what made that noise, as the satellite phone had become one with the pilothouse. Leah put her hand in my pocket to produce my new cell phone. "Allo," she said, then "M. Lemaire wants to speak to you urgently."

He's heard about the fire, I thought. As soon as I spoke the phone unleashed a rapid stream of excited French. "M. Lemaire, please slow down, I can't understand a word."

"You must help, we must find it."

"What, what have you lost? And please, speak slowly or you'll lose me."

"An object, the Airforce, that is to say Terreau, nous, have lost an object in the sea. You find it for us."

"M. Lemaire, I have some bad news for you. A saboteur has burned our ship, I don't know if we can help. Haven't you got a navy? Side scan sonar? Magnetometers?"

"Non, non, you understand not. This object is under the sea in a busy channel, waves, many ships, people. On the bottom are many things like it. We need Dr. Jenkins. Please." His English had got down to the level of my French.

A suspicion grew in my mind. "Would this object be a metal cylinder, very heavy, about three meters long, a meter diameter?"

"Yes, no, I can't tell you. We must find it, nobody must know. The navy, no one."

"M. Lemaire, for the amity of nations if nothing else, we would be honored to help, but our boat is burned. We don't know how much is left of the apparatus. The hydraphones are intact, but the electronics . . . "

"Fixed, it must be fixed. People, I send our best people, Dr. Jenkins will direct them, tonight we start."

"Wait, I'll talk to Dr Jenkins." I covered the mouthpiece to give Joe the news.

"I think they've lost a nuclear bomb in the sea somewhere under a busy traffic lane, in a port by the sound of it. They want us to find it before anything bad happens. Lemaire says he'll send a crew to start work tonight."

William reminded us of something important. "We don't have any sort of contract with them, we can't have a whole crew from Terreau build a new Finder."

Joe sat shaking his head. We waited for him to decide if it could be done. After a minute's meditation he said, "Get the crew together tonight to plan the job. We'll meet on the Mela to look at what's left."

I uncovered the mouthpiece. "Dr Jenkins is willing to try, wants some engineers to meet him at the boat to assess the damage." I covered the mouthpiece again. "Francois?" I asked

Joe. He nodded. "Send Joe's college friend, they've worked together before. But," a groan came distinctly over the phone, "we don't have a contract. You were to give us an answer tomorrow. How can we share all the technology without some agreement?"

"The deal you said today, is that still your offer?"

"Yes, of course. We'll throw the work on this problem of yours in as a gesture of amity."

"Accepted. You have my word on it. Now I start getting my people together. Secrecy of course, most of them won't know why they are doing this."

"Get going Joe, take Leah to interpret. Terreau agrees to the hundred million."

Well, that line got a good reception. My crew stood like statues for a moment, then was all over me. Kissing and hugging, enough to give me delusions of adequacy.

The workers were bundled off in a cab with instructions to remember to sleep sometime. William still looked doubtful. I reassured him, "Tomorrow we'll visit Terreau to get at least a memo of understanding. I think they're really frightened. I'm not sure why, that sort of bomb doesn't arm just because you drop it, it has to have a separate go signal. I wonder what went wrong."

Joe and Leah hadn't come back by the start of the business day so Mary as secretary of the day set up appointments with Terreau. William and Mike went off to the legal department, Mike with instructions to try to look like a member of the board of a multi-million dollar corporation. I visited a haggard M. Lemaire who had evidently been up all night. I asked him what agitated him so much about the 'object.' After all, it isn't armed, right? He gave me an ominous reply.

"Normally what you say is very true, the object is safe to drop. In this case the support aircraft carried an experimental new launch platform. There was an accident to the wiring, a fire did considerable damage, the plane barely survived. My advisors are of the opinion the object is probably not armed."

Wrong word to use about a nuclear warhead. *"Probably?"* I croaked.

He nodded. "I see you understand the gravity of the situation." He certainly looked as if he did.

I realized the extra dimension his worry had. "The new launch platform, it was a Terreau product?"

Instead of answering he put his head in his hands and said something about the guillotine.

"Oh now, M. Lemaire, I'm sure it won't come to that. We'll make sure the object is safely recovered. Without undue publicity. Of course, if we fail we'll be among the first to know. I think we should move our ship to a facility which can start repairing the navigation equipment as soon as possible."

He cheered up slightly at this, told me he had taken the liberty of having the boat towed up the Seine to get the repairs started. I jumped up to rush off to supervise the yard, knowing even a hundred million isn't enough for a boatyard left to themselves to decide what work is needed. He insisted on coming with me, so we rode in style in the company limo. The limo saved a considerable taxi ride, as there aren't any shipyards in Paris.

Joe and his crew were busy in the stern house. When I asked him how he liked being out in the country he wanted to know what I was talking about, unaware he had been moved out of Paris. I left them to it. Leah had cleaned up the salon as best she could, still streaked with smoke as it was. A new carpet would definitely be needed. The parrot had unfortunately inhaled more smoke than its delicate constitution could handle and had been given decent burial. M. Lemaire wanted to talk to his crew, so Leah and I went to interview the yard manager. We impressed on him the need for a quick minimum repair, seaworthy, with the minimum essential navigation gear but forget replacing the computer. A new pilothouse would have to be built, but plain marine plywood, no mahogany. The deck had to come up too, burned almost through to the cabins. I insisted he get a naval architect to design the new construction, as we need to take the boat to sea. Caterpillar could easily supply a complete new set of engine instruments. "How many day's work?" I asked after the specifications were written down.

"Months you mean," Leah translated.

"Tell him three crews, twenty four hours a day, seven days a week. If he needs stimulating say we'll have the government here to supervise."

A lot of 'impossible' was exchanged. M. Lemaire came up to help. The only word I understood was "Attention!" Leah explained Lemaire had said he'd buy the yard and fire everyone in it if it didn't get done in a matter of days. And get an income tax audit in. I think it was that last threat which got the workers pulling apart the remains of the pilothouse off before we left.

Leah looked regretfully at the devastation. "Pity about Natasha's article, all burned up in the computer."

"Oh hell, I left the discs in my dirty shirt. They'll get washed. I copied the article before we went to Terreau. Now it's lost."

"Oh, that's what they are. I took them out of your pocket before the laundry went. They're in a drawer with my pants."

I kissed her. "I don't know what we would have done without you, Leah. The Mela Corporation owes you a whole lot."

"And they're going to make good on it too, in diamonds, remember?"

M. Lemaire joined us on the walk back to the limo through the clutter of discarded boat parts. I asked him rather an important question. "By the way, what port is the object lost in?"

He muttered the answer so low I barely caught it. I took the liberty of grabbing him by the arm. "I think we should find a quiet place to sit while you tell me *all* about it."

He looked at Leah. "Votre maitresse, should she be burdened with all this?"

I got in slightly ahead of Leah. "Mademoiselle is not my mistress, she is a trusted colleague. I value her advice highly." Dammit, he had me talking broken English.

We sat on an upside down dinghy that had seen better days. "Now, monsieur, the whole truth. The port you mentioned is not a French port, is that not so?" He nodded. "So," I went on, "if we should set off the object that is 'probably' not armed, if they don't still use the guillotine in France they will probably revive it just for the management of Terreau CSF. Of course, we won't be there to join you, as we will have been vaporized earlier. Along with one of the principle cities of a friendly neighbor."

He added a further cheery note to this scenario. "If it doesn't go off, which is most probable, but our neighbor learns of the incident, we will instead all spend considerable time in one of our penal colonies. The guillotine might be preferable."

Chapter 12

You will have noticed that I have not told you the name of the port in which M. Lemaire's 'object' nestled, armed or not as the case might be. In fact, Lemaire never actually admitted in so many words that it was a bomb. I think the reasons for this reticence are obvious. No names no penal colony, if you see what I mean.

I sat with my face in my hands thinking about the pickle we were in. It occurred to me that there had been a lot of sitting in this attitude recently, and not just by me. The hundred million didn't seem sufficient compensation at that moment. Leah interrupted my meditation by asking the question that was uppermost in my mind too.

"But monsieur, when we find your object for you, what then? It surely must be quite heavy, tons I should think. What are we to do? Fish for it with a magnet on a string? Teleport it to the surface?"

I introduced another aspect of the problem, as if we needed one. "All the ship's papers are burned up. To enter a foreign port we need registry, clearance, all sorts of things. I don't know if they can be got in a hurry, we have to contact the US Coast Guard in Portland Oregon, on the other side of the US."

Lemaire looked as if he wanted to bury his face in his hands too but resisted the urge. "Papers we can solve, I call some friends in the ministry. As to raising the object, it only weighs a few thousand kilos, surely you sailors can manage that somehow. No?"

"In a busy ship channel without anyone seeing what we're doing? M. Lemaire, miracles are beyond us. However, I'll get all of the Mela crew together to think about it. I can see why you can't send the French navy to do it, even if they could find it. I suppose your concern with the possibility of penal colonies is because you and your confederates in the air force should have reported this accident to the government when it happened? And didn't?"

"Confederates?" Leah supplied the French equivalent. He nodded. "Quite so."

We all three put our faces in our hands and sat for a while in gloomy meditation.

The five of us left over convened in my suite to exchange the day's news. Mike and William had been spectacularly successful. They had got the money deposited in three Cayman Island banks at two percent per annum interest, which William apologized for but said it was the best he could get short term. The interest would be wired to Mela Corporation's Paris bank account, opened for the purpose. I thought about two percent. "That's a hundred and sixty-seven thousand a month," I gasped.

"Well, we have expenses and French and US taxes. I doubt if there'll be more than a few thousand a month left for each of us. Mike and I have looked at rentals, we'd like to take something where we can all live in comfort, get maid service, perhaps a staff. We need cars of our own too, we can rent them wholesale."

The group heartily approved this plan. I thought I heard someone murmur something about diamonds. I suggested we take time out for dinner, then reconvene to work on the little problem M. Lemaire had set us. As we were leaving the phone beeped. Leah answered in the persona of secretary. After a rapid exchange she covered the microphone to tell us it was Lemaire's secretary calling, asking if she could come to visit the distinguished doctor Jenkins. "Tell her," I said, "that Dr Jenkins is on the Mermaid, at the boatyard. If she wants to meet him she might drive over, see if she can get him to eat and take a rest."

Leah told her, switched the phone off, and went into a fit of giggles. "She just said 'Ooooh' and hung up."

Wherever the distinguished Dr Jenkins may have rested that night it wasn't in his hotel room.

There were two camps at dinner. One, innocent of what Lemaire had sprung on us, made a celebration out of it. The other, consisting of Leah and I, was thoughtful and grave. When we were settled with drinks back in the hotel in the sitting room of my suite I explained what we had to do. The whole party became thoughtful and grave. William had a solution. "Give the money back."

Rejected four to one.

Mike murmured something we didn't catch. Speak up, we urged, anything's worth discussing.

"I just thought it's a pity there isn't a miniature Glomar Explorer."

For those of you too young to remember, the Glomar Explorer stole a sunken Russian submarine for the CIA. It had a floodable hold in which the bottom opened so the catch could be hauled up inside the ship. Much too big for our job, and too well known, if she still existed.

"Well," said Mary, "build a little one."

Leah had a cogent objection. "But if the middle is open everybody would see what we've hauled up, and the whole idea is it's got to be secret. What would you pretend it was if it had a great windowless room in the middle of it?"

"Thank you everybody," I said. "I'll sketch it out tomorrow at Terreau, they can build it."

I wasn't allowed to get away with that. "OK, OK, shut up and I'll explain. We get a small barge, load it with diving gear and a couple of divers from the military. Lemaire seems to be able to arrange about anything. In the bottom we put two valves, like you might use to flood it. They'll be capped off and closed for inspection. We make two pipes that screw into the valves and come up well above the waterline. At each end of the barge we put a rubber dinghy hanging from a nice strong electric crane. To recover the object, assuming we find it, assuming it doesn't go bang, we swivel the cranes round and lower the cables through the pipes, with a snap hook on the end to fit the lugs on the object. The divers go down to inspect interesting wrecks, snap the hooks onto the thing, we haul it up so it snugs against the underside of the barge. Some tarps lashed over the cranes, deliver the results of the 'antique wreck survey' cover story to the local museum, take off slowly on a long tow to meet a salvage ship out beyond territorial waters. They hoist barge, bomb, divers and all aboard, we take off at hull speed to receive the thanks of a grateful republic. Except there won't be any, everybody will pretend it never happened."

Absolutely crazy was the unanimous opinion. As was the vote to do it. William had a question. "Why a long tow slowly? If it goes off the length of the tow won't help us. Unless the cable's twenty miles long."

"Because I think the further away it is from the turbulence and vibration of the propeller the better."

Carried, nem con.

A horrid thought suddenly came to me. "Natasha and Mikel, they'll come back to no home, they won't know where we've gone."

Mary and Leah volunteered to wait on the embankment when the pair was due back. Didn't sound much fun to me, but perhaps they had in mind to try their game on passing Frenchmen.

I thought it kinder to wait until the morning to approach Lemaire with our new project. He was definitely showing the strain, perhaps a good night's sleep would bring the roses back to his cheeks. But I doubted it. I spent a busy morning with Lemaire's mechanical engineering department. We got along in a mixture of French, English, and innumerable sketches. Before lunch the design appeared in their cad-cam system as an experimental positioning system for divers. I'm happy to say that most of those who worked on this project have no idea to this day what it was for. Minions were dispatched up and down the Seine and connecting waterways to find a suitable barge, while Lemaire and I went to lunch in a slightly more cheerful frame of mind. The rest of the Mela Corporation had disappeared on some complicated errand saying they'd be back by evening. I checked that I had my bankcard safely back in my wallet.

When we straggled back to the hotel at the end of a busy day there was a package waiting at the desk for me. I took it up to read at leisure. Mike, William, and the girls, had had a very busy afternoon. They had rented an office, furnished it, installed telephones and a computer, hired a receptionist, and sent the address to our various banks and business associates. I congratulated them on a really good day's work. Leah opened the package while they talked. When William had finished she started describing the contents. First was a set of papers showing the Mela Mermaid had been reborn fully documented as the navire de recherches "Belle Celestine" of Paris, France, nominal owner Terreau CSF, on indefinite lease to the Mela Corporation. The rest of the package contained papers certifying that, having passed all the required examinations with the highest marks and completed the necessary time at sea demonstrating to a high degree the qualities necessary in a prudent mariner, I was now a licensed master mariner under European Economic Union rules.

Now I do like people round me to be happy, but really, rolling on the floor laughing their silly heads off repeating to each other 'prudent mariner, ahahahaha' at the tops of their voices was entirely uncalled for, and hurtful to my feelings. They even referred to that old unfortunate adventure in Alaska as part of the joke. Our plan to go fishing for a nuclear bomb in a high traffic area of a foreign port came into it too.

"Quiet," I yelled, "the whole hotel will hear you."

Under the circumstances I thought it fair we should all get the same wages, one thousand euros a week each. The new bookkeeper of the Mela Corporation took care of that, with deductions for taxes for two nations. That's not as bad as it sounds because the US tax credits the foreign tax against the bill. Our Paris office developed into a real workplace, though there wasn't much to do yet.

The Belle Celestine and its barge didn't get rebuilt in a few days of course, but they did get done in two weeks including a coat of paint. I thought M. Lemaire would lose his mind with impatience and worry by the end of it.

The core of the Finder is the computer. Smoke and flame were not kind to the Sun, but Terreau had one of their own which worked almost as well. Joe fortunately kept complete duplicate software in his cabin, unburned, including each update he'd made. Francois rebuilt the custom parallel processor, whatever that might be, while a gang of ladies from one of Terreau's plants rewired the laboratory. Finished it looked a lot neater than before the fire. The box in which the pictures appear took the most time and effort to rebuild, particularly as nobody but Joe understood how it worked. I'll give you a sample of Francois trying.

"But Joe, I still don't see how your second algorithm recovers the phase information from the de-convolution of the first image transform."

I bet you don't either.

Two extremely tough looking divers joined us to plan the expedition, seconded from 'a government department.' Leah, Natasha and I made a trip to what between ourselves we referred to as 'direct ground zero,' a joke M. Lemaire did not find at all amusing. There we gave the city museum a tremendous pitch on surveying the waters outside the port to photograph and map the local wrecks, as part of the test cycle of a new underwater survey device. We played Natasha's article for them without details on the mechanism, which had them practically drooling with eagerness for the survey to start. We were happy, we told them, to hand all the results over to them, as we were only interested in the device, not the archeology. They understood perfectly that we needed to send divers down to confirm some sightings, but we assured them we had no intention of raising anything, just surveying. They actually called the port captain and the mayor in to see our pictures, so we became honored visitors to whom they were all grateful for the free work. Of course, I promised to avoid interfering with the commercial traffic of the port, but as they must understand our research vessel had necessarily to move slowly to avoid damaging our equipment. The port captain therefore issued a local notice to mariners warning them of our innocent presence among them, very helpful of him. A great pity, I thought to myself, if our mission should have the worst possible outcome. All these nice helpful people blowing away in a radioactive cloud. With our atoms among them.

Chapter 13

The Ugly Duckling, the informal name of our little barge, had several design improvements over the original concept. Two steel beams welded along the bottom to distribute the weight of The Object, as we now referred to it, and to keep the barge from folding in the middle while being lifted from the water. A fitting in the crane cables so they could be disconnected from the load to return to their innocent pose as dinghy launchers. A very convincing air tank recharging station obscuring one of the recovery fittings, a small generator to power the barge the other. All in all a very believable cover for our clandestine operation. Grapnels, anchors, chain, coils of rope, all added verisimilitude. The divers did some rehearsals at dead of night with a dummy Object, worked like a charm. In nice calm water a few feet deep of course. They did the rehearsals in the dark to simulate the conditions at the spot where The Object was presumed to rest in murky turbid water.

Selecting the crew for the undertaking took two days of acrimonious dispute and hurt feelings. Joe had to go to work the Finder, Mike and I to manage the boat. William had to stay behind to provide legal assistance if we should manage to displease the local authorities. Natasha and Mikel were essential to our cover story. William wanted to come, M. Lemaire wanted Joe not to. I strongly urged we leave the girls out of this extremely hazardous expedition with its slight chance of getting vaporized and strong possibility of spending substantial jail time. Eventually we reached an amicable compromise satisfactory to almost all parties. William stayed behind.

We got two skilled canal pilots, a police escort, permission to run at night, special treatment at the locks, in fact everything Lemaire with Terreau CSF behind him could think of to speed us to the Ocean and our rendezvous with fate. Watching the pilots, cigarettes dangling from the side of their mouths, one hand in the pocket, gave me a whole new appreciation for the skill needed in an inland mariner. The Ugly Duckling followed on a short tow, narrowly missing bridge abutments, other traffic, mud flats, pilings, buoys, and people's riverside gardens, with hardly a glance behind from the pilot. Agitated cries of "Monsieur, have a care. Mind the transducer arrays on the lock gate" and the like perturbed them not at all as the Belle Celestine rushed headlong through narrow tortuous passages.

We dropped the pilots and police escort at tidal waters to make the sea passage. The autumn sea had considerable lumps in it, not what we were used to on rivers and canals. Towing is easy if the cable is the right length and you are careful not to let it pull taut, which will surely break it. Easy in calm water, more difficult in a rising sea. Breaking the cable would have two untoward effects. We would be forced to try to recover the tow without getting the dangling ends of the cable wrapped round the propeller, bad enough, but much more serious was the presence of Joe's laboratory on the aft deck in line with the potential recoil of the broken end. I impressed on Joe that he absolutely mustn't go in his hut while we were towing at speed. Seven knots doesn't sound very fast but the drag behind us made it flat out, requiring concentration equivalent to driving a racecar.

To come into the inner harbor a prudent mariner would tie the barge alongside, not trail it in a sweep of destruction through the port. This proved a lot more difficult than I expected. Joe's hut left only a tiny rear deck to manage the cable, and to get to it one had to hang onto a rail round the outside of the hut. If we had to do this in a seaway I could see someone getting drowned. Hanging over the operation would also be the ever-present danger of getting the cable in the propeller. Well, too late now to change the design.

We had dinner ashore with some of the museum staff. Mikel and Natasha told stories of expeditions they had been on, the museum people told us the history of the port, what we should expect to find, and where they were most interested in exploring. I invited a few to join us for our first sweep, doing everything in fact I would have if the survey were really what we were here for.

We didn't need the Ugly Duckling for the initial survey, so left it moored. There was yet, after all, nothing on it to rouse suspicion that we might not be what we seemed. The bottom of the harbor channel, and the bay outside, were absolutely littered with the remains of hundreds of years of commerce and war. Unexploded bombs, airplanes from at least three countries, fishing boats, some quite large ships, strange things lost from cargoes of all ages. Fascinating. One strange thing had us puzzled until someone recognized it as a steam locomotive upside down.

Our visitors had the standard stunned reaction to their first sight of the Finder, tried to touch the image, called it the invention of the century, the usual stuff Joe lapped up. Mikel took discs full of photos, now automatically labeled with the GPS position appearing as a row of neat block letters along the bottom of the display. One of the most interesting and mysterious sights we came across consisted of a row of cannon, right under the reserved ship lane. The arrangement suggested a large wooden warship had rotted away on its side there, leaving the cannon to mark its grave. Against this theory the museum people couldn't think of any ship which it might be. Joe gave them the best picture he could of the cannons, with the idea that an expert might be able to date them.

We no longer had any way to store or display Mikel's pictures now the pilothouse computer had gone to the great recycle bin in the sky, so Mikel gave all the discs to the museum, in exchange for a promise of prints off some of them. We promised them more, together with anything interesting the divers might see when we got down to the serious business of systematically testing the equipment. What we didn't see was anything identifiable as The Object. There were plenty of things like it as M. Lemaire had said, but nothing the right size in the channel where he said it was.

Once the visitors were ashore we settled grimly down to a systematic search. The finder worked just as well at night as in daylight of course. GPS positions meant we didn't need visual references. We did however need a constant lookout to see which of the mass of lights round us were moving. Three days of staring into the display in eight-hour watches took some of the edge off our enthusiasm. The counter-sway of the display to the rolling of the boat became particularly disquieting as the water got rough outside. Some watchers had to have a bowl beside them.

I called M. Lemaire to see if he could improve on the position that he had given us. A difficult conversation over an insecure phone. He talked to the aircrew responsible for all this, without coming up with anything useful. We all got so tired and frazzled that I decided that a run ashore, restaurant food, perhaps beds which didn't sway might be a good idea. Even the two divers agreed. It was cold and foggy in the early morning when we came back. Nobody felt like climbing about with numb fingers on slippery decks to raise the transducer arrays out of the water so I agreed we could leave them down just this once, I'd be especially careful not to hit anything with them. Joe stayed in the hut, too tired and discouraged to come out until the boat became stationary with fresh coffee making.

Once everything was secure and the engine shut down we gathered in the salon for a post mortem, coffee with just a little brandy in it all round. Joe came out to join us with rather an odd look on his face. He waited for coffee before speaking.

"Well Joe," I asked, "what else can we do?"

"Ah, well," he said thoughtfully, "I think we've been looking in the wrong place altogether."

"What makes you say that, Joe?"

"Because it's right underneath us, here in the mooring. We never ran the finder here before."

Now I know we had been living for weeks with the knowledge we were going to tangle with a nuclear bomb of dubious reliability, but there's something immediate about being told it's twenty-five feet below the chair you're sitting in. Considerably more brandy got added to the coffee. I stopped the incipient rush to the Finder, instead sent Joe back with the two divers who knew exactly what The Object looked like. They returned in a few minutes, the two of them displaying more animation than we had seen so far. I think one of them almost smiled.

"Vraiment."

I returned his usual somber mood by pointing out the obvious. "That's very good, we've found it. Now how do we get it? This area's lit up at night like an operating room, there aren't even any shadows. There are people all round, police, coastguard, probably legions of spies, crews from every country you can think of. It's going to be difficult to be surreptitious about working the cranes, putting divers over, running cables up and down. I can't think of a cover story for all that, including running the cables through the bottom of the boat. That's not one of those routine operations you see every day."

Mary had the proper attitude. She burst into tears.

Brandy is good, but for real thought one needs Chivas Regal. It had all gone. I determined to get more even if I had to fly to Scotland to do it. We did our best with the brandy.

Mike, who frequently comes up with good idea but is weak on putting them into practice, asked an interesting question. "What's the weather forecast?"

I walked up the stairs to the pilothouse to hear from the weather channel. Which was in a language I didn't understand. One of the divers did though. Foggy in the morning, burning off early. "Very good, Mike, what else do you suggest?"

"Put the dinghy anchor over the side with a float on the end. Jiggle it about until Joe says it's almost touching The Object, so the divers can go straight to it. Fold up the hydraphones, bring the Ugly Duckling alongside so the divers can clean the bottoms of both boats. Get the cables rigged and down in the fog, should only take a few minutes. If we can get the job done with the cranes back to their usual position before the fog lifts we're in. The tarp covers everything up so the pipes won't show. Then take off to sea as soon as we can."

"We need clearance to leave port for good."

"Get rid of The Object at sea and come back for clearance, they don't know we're not out surveying."

Mary stopped crying.

I called the port to let them know we'd be flying a dive flag for the bottom work in the morning, but the divers would not be away from the immediate vicinity so there was no hazard. They thanked me for the information with an exchange of courtesies. Such nice people. I did hope they would all be alive by the end of tomorrow.

Putting the boat anchor down and adjusted while pretending to tidy the docklines and fenders just took nerve, working from Joe's instructions whispered in a chain from the hut. Actually I dropped it right on the Object. I could feel the clang through my whole body, found I'd bitten my tongue hard enough to draw blood. I did wish we still had some Chivas.

The morning early was beautifully dark and foggy. We worked frantically to get the job done before the day warmed up without making a lot of suspicious noises. The divers each held one crane cable while they worked their way down the boat anchor rode to the Object. They had to find the lugs by touch but they'd practiced that. Fortunately it was lying on its side so the lugs were accessible. Two jerks on each cable told us they were secure, the cranes whined, the cable came reeling in smooth as silk. A ribbon tied to the cable showed when the lift neared the bottom of the barge, the load edged up to nest between the girders with the lugs fitted into sockets provided to hold the load in place. The keys went into the cable fittings to fix them, and the workers breathed for the first time in minutes. The cranes were back to their rightful position in a second, the tarp lashed down, everyone back on the Celestine in good order. Slick as can be. The fog lifted to disclose to the world that our divers were cleaning the boat bottoms. Peace and security reigned.

Chapter 14

The divers climbed onto their barge to shed their gear. When they were dressed for company again breakfast was served in the salon while I laid out the day's itinerary.

"I am not going to hand this thing over in daylight," I told them, "so we have to spend the day off just as we planned. Everybody but an anchor watch will go ashore. Shopping, sightseeing, a little lunch. Act casual. Mikel and Natasha, perhaps you could visit our friends at the museum, give them the rest of the discs. Let drop we've finished our tests, another day or two and we'll be leaving. Straggle back here between three and four, and try not to look like rangers going on a suicide mission when you do." I looked at the divers. "Perhaps you wish to go somewhere private and contact your organization?"

"One of us will stay, the other go." Not exactly chatty, secret agents, as I presumed they were.

The water taxi took us right downtown, and if that tells you where we were I deny it. Our diver vanished like a shadow, the archeology team set off for the museum, Mike and Mary disappeared hand in hand in the direction of the expensive shops. "What," I asked Leah, "would you like to do on your day off?" So we spent the day being tourists on a sightseeing bus.

By four the crew was back on board. The divers climbed onto the barge to look like a survey team, ready to tend lines and slings at our rendezvous, and Mary's parcels were out of the salon into her cabin. Mike dropped the mooring and the Belle Celestine with Ugly Duckling towing dutifully alongside set off to sea exuding innocence. Once out of the harbor the barge settled back to the end of its towline, not, I thought, noticeably lower in the water than she had been the night before. I can't say I relaxed, but I did breath normally for a few minutes.

Looking back at the towline in the mirror placed so the helmsman could see the bight of the cable I saw a local coast guard cutter frothing busily up behind us, the gun on her foredeck making her look quite like a little battleship. We were well to the right of the channel leaving plenty of room for her to pass so I concentrated on the traffic ahead.

The radio suddenly spoke. "Belle Celestine," it squawked, "return to port immediately. You are wanted on shore." I looked left to see the cutter pacing us.

Some Roman whose name I forget once said he always agreed with Caesar, because 'it is ill to argue with the master of a thousand legions.' It is similarly ill to argue with the master of a 90mm rapid-fire naval rifle. "Yes sir," I said, "but I can't turn the tow here. Then I need to bring the barge back alongside."

"Go to dead slow and wait," came the uncompromising order. A white uniformed crew dressed in red life jackets piled into a large inflatable to rush across to us and swarm onto the barge and the stern of the Celestine to manage the cable. In a flash it seemed the barge was back tied alongside, the inflatable was back on the cutter, and the radio was instructing me to make the turn "now."

My crew all crowded into the pilothouse making it almost impossible to manage the helm. I sent them away with instructions to look innocent, not like a captured pirate crew. Not that I thought it would do any good, we were caught good and proper.

A smart pinnace came alongside as soon as we picked up the mooring. Two seamen with sidearms came aboard to shepherd us all onto the pinnace. One of them stayed in the pilothouse, the other stood on the foredeck. 'Goodbye, Mela Mermaid,' I thought sadly, 'it's been fun.'

A minibus waited on the quay to take us away. We were driven in silence through the city, to a building with a broad flight of stone steps. We were ushered out of the bus up the stairs, which I suddenly recognized. Various exclamations of surprise and dismay escaped my companions as we entered the huge main door of the city museum. "Now what the hell are we doing here?" Mike wanted to know.

A burst of applause greeted us. The museum director, beaming all over his face, came forward to shake our hands. "Welcome, welcome, to the opening of the 'Belle Celestine' exhibition." Leah held my arm to avoid collapsing. He led us to a gallery with a magnificent display of Mikel's photos, enlarged with descriptions in three languages of the wonders we had found. The museum's collection of marine relics occupied cases round the gallery, some of them actually connected to the pictures. Tables of what has been called 'bait on crackers' occupied the center of the room with, I was very happy to see, ample champagne.

"You all look stunned," remarked the director still beaming.

"We are overwhelmed by the honor, totally unexpected as it is." He didn't know how true that was. "On behalf of the crew I thank you and everyone who put on this magnificent display. Truly a memorable event for us." Also a more sincere sentiment than he could have guessed.

A vivid mental picture came to me of The Object hanging below the barge, now in the charge of two coast guards with sidearms. I found I was sweating more than the temperature of the room required. Leah still clutched my arm. "Stop biting your lip," I whispered to her, "enjoy the reception." I won't tell you what she whispered back, not at all ladylike.

I set off to tour the exhibition. On the way I came across Mary circling the champagne table. I inquired how she was enjoying the party. "I wet my pants when they ordered us off the bus," she confided, "I left them in the lady's room."

This is a difficult conversational opening to reply to. None of the conventional answers seem appropriate. Instead I said, "be careful with that stuff, it creeps up on you." She also whispered something unladylike. I passed on to admire the pictures. At one of them I came across a very old man leaning on a cane studying the scene intently. "Do you happen to know how that locomotive came to be at the bottom of the ship channel?" I asked.

"Oh yes, I remember it well. My father once ran that loco. The Germans were taking it away on a barge, but someone had removed a vital pin which should have kept it from sliding off the barge." He chuckled. "My father gave me that pin as a memento of how he helped win the war. He and I went up on the hill to watch the barge leave. Even from there it made a fine splash."

"How interesting," I told him, "we wondered how it got there. Thank you for telling me. You must have been very young at the time."

"Yes, yes, it's all a very long time ago. See how the boiler has rusted almost away. Now the Germans are our friends we are told and I too am rusting away. The pin is in that case over there, I lent it to the museum for this occasion." In the case rested a massive steel coupling pin with a note on its history. I wandered off to look at the rest of the pictures. Part way round an officer in a uniform I didn't recognize approached me. He handed me an envelope. "We have taken the liberty of keeping you from your work for this whole evening when I know you wanted to be at sea." You don't know how much we wanted to be I thought. "I have therefore prepared your clearance papers so you may leave when ever you are ready without troubling to come to the customs station."

"Now that is very thoughtful of you," I said with real sincerity, "We are anxious to complete our last test and get back to Paris. We will always be grateful for the kindness and hospitality shown us here." And that it was still here, so far anyway.

The affair eventually ended, after what seemed to me like hours and hours. We were escorted down to the bus Mike and I supporting Mary, on whom the champagne had indeed crept up, back on the pinnace, and onto the Belle Celestine covered with kisses, hand shakes, pats on the back, and the girls told me later several unexpected pinches. The coast guard saluted and left.

The crew collapsed on to chairs and cushions with a collective sigh of relief. Except for Mary who had gone straight to sleep, still I presume pantless, where we had dropped her. Even the divers looked shaken. "There," I said, "wasn't that fun?" My crew growled at me. "Now," I continued, "as soon as we're pulled together we're going out for night exercises."

Leah announced "I'm going to throw up now," and left for her cabin. Mikel and Natasha went down to theirs to sleep it off.

It took a few minutes to persuade Mike I really meant it. Even a reminder of what we had swinging about under the barge didn't raise what you might call enthusiasm. I started the engine, the dive party jumped down on the barge to put on their wet suits, and Mike went reluctantly out to cast off the mooring. We waved back to people on the quay on our way to a rendezvous twenty-five miles out to sea. The waves in the channel were quite high, giving the barge crew trouble getting the tow cable out. I didn't know how exactly we were going to get the barge out of the water if it got really rough. Dropping The Object again in deep water would not make a happy end to the day. My instructions were to say one word on channel 72 to announce we were at sea, no reply expected. I picked up the microphone, said "Mermaid" into it, waited for a minute for some sign anyone was listening, and went back to channel 16. The lights of the port faded behind us, the sea rose until sometimes the barge appeared outlined against the clouds above us. I slowed down to a couple of knots. "Mike," I asked between clenched teeth, "turn the searchlight back on the cable so I can see what I'm doing." On the whole I felt happier before he did it. Scary.

Half an hour of this convinced me the tow would not break if I were careful, the Celestine was seaworthy enough for much worse weather than this, the barge didn't seem to be shipping water, and twelve hours to reach the rendezvous in full daylight next morning wouldn't do. I edged the throttle forward a little at a time, watching the cable. The bight pulled up out of the water occasionally, but it looked safe enough. Besides, we'd used a cable much stronger than would normally be needed for this light a tow. The GPS screen reflected my optimism by ticking down the time-to-go from 12 to 8 to 5 hours. Fine, except the sweat made my eyes smart.

After an interminable run in the dark with one pee break leaving a rigid Mike at the wheel we got a radar return from the appointed spot. I tried the radio again.

"Mermaid?" I said wistfully.

"Good evening captain," came back a hearty voice with a French accent, "we've been expecting you for some time."

"Yes, well, we were somewhat delayed by the port authorities. I expect the people who must be having rather a bad time on the barge will tell you all about it when, or perhaps if, you get them aboard."

"The sea is a bit sloppy, but I'm sure we'll have no problem."

Good, I thought, wish I were. At that moment a sea came right over our bows, sloshed back along the deck to break on the makeshift pilothouse, shaking it alarmingly. "See you in about two hours," I called back.

In slightly less than that estimate we came up to a very odd vessel. The front of her looked like any other bridge-forward ship, but behind the funnel she was as it were cut down, leaving a flat steel deck only about ten feet above the water. Right at the stern she mounted a crane big enough to lift the Celestine out of the water. She flew no ensign, but her name showed in white on her bows in the reflection of her searchlights in the water. 'Salvor' which I thought very appropriate. My job was to maneuver the Ugly Duckling under the crane so the divers could pull two huge slings under the barge. The crane would then haul her up by brute force, restrained by guy wires from the slings to crews on the deck. Easy in calm water, but here the Celestine and barge were surging back and forward at random while rising and falling ten feet or more not in unison. I tried. Twice the Celestine hit the huge hull beside us with a splintering crash that boded well for the financial future of our boatyard, if we survived to reach it. One hit like that could easily sink the barge, leaving all the weary work to do over in water two thousand meters deep. I called the captain. "This is much too dangerous, think what we've got hanging under that barge. We can't do it in this sea. What do you suggest?"

"Wait one," came the answer. I dropped back clear of the Salvor to recover. All the warning lights had been left off the dash in the hurry to get the boat back in service, so the bilge pumps could come on unannounced. In the lull while I waited I heard them cycling on and off. Oh well, we could always hitch a ride back on the ship. The radio came to life.

"Come up at a safe distance in our lee," it instructed, "I will assist you."

Before I had time to ask how the hell they planned to do that, an enormous rigid hull inflatable with two huge outboards on it came frothing round the stern of the Salvor. It backed up to the barge, fixed a cable to the stern, and towed it by brute force through the slings hanging in the sea from the crane while I held it off the steel hull of the Salvor with the tow cable. The divers hauled in the tow cable, which I rushed back to release, making the precarious trip round Joe's hut in record time. The crane then hoisted the barge, divers, Object and all, swinging into the air. The crane swung round, the crew on deck hauled in the guy wires, and the Ugly Duckling settled gently onto a cradle in the middle of the low deck. Mike and I watched with our mouths hanging open. The inflatable rushed back to get itself hauled up, the captain called "Goodbye, thanks," on the radio and the ship accelerated into the night leaving us rolling and pitching in its wake.

"Just shows what you can do with the right equipment," Mike remarked.

Chapter 15

I collected my thoughts to concentrate on my poor boat. Switch off the towing lights. Switch off the searchlight. Direct the GPS to produce a compass course to the port where we could slide into the peace of the canals. Set the autopilot to the indicated course. Mourn the burned computer that would have done most of this for me. Run the engine up to the fastest I thought the boat could stand. Try to relax.

Our new pilothouse did not do well under the stress of waves coming aboard, the wind driven rain, and the motion of the boat. The rain and spray came in round the windows, the sea came in under the walls, the roof leaked. An hour of this had the deck in the pilothouse as wet as that outside. When I touched the dash I got an electric shock. The seawater had got in the high voltage wiring. Before I had time to decide what to do about it a loud bang came from somewhere in the boat. Several gauges on the dash went to zero.

"What the hell was that?" asked Mike on a note of panic.

"I think that was the ground fault protector shutting the generator down," I told him, "so we don't get electrocuted. No problem, everything important runs on twenty-four volts off the engine."

We ploughed on, cold, almost as wet as if we'd been on deck, tired, and suffering the letdown of a completed mission. The champagne had long ago worn off. Coffee would have been most welcome, but the pot worked on the now dead hundred and ten volts, even if one of us had felt like making it. I suggested Mike should go on an inspection tour of the boat, then get some rest for an hour to relieve me to do the same. He came back five minutes later with a report.

"Water spurts into the engine room each time we roll to starboard, trickles in the rest of the time. The pump is managing. Nothing we can do about it anyway. Without the generator there's no heat in the cabins, people are cold, damp, miserable, and blaming you and I. I'm going to bed now." With which cheery bulletin he left me.

Dawn came with a lightening of the clouds but no sun in sight. I had been sitting on the wet helm seat dozing, as Mike had never returned. Leah appeared, ashen faced with green accents. "Good god," she said, "have you been sitting in the wet by yourself all fucking night?"

I nodded. The Celestine chose that moment to trip so she buried her bows in the wave instead of rising to it. The wave surged back along the foredeck to break on the pilothouse. Water swirled in through the bottom seams over Leah's feet. Her "Eeeek" seemed the appropriate response to me.

"Come on down to the salon, I'll get you a drink. The boat can look after itself."

I reluctantly informed her there was no electricity any more.

"I know that, the cabins are like ice boxes. Won't the propane still work?"

Of course it would. I let myself be led below, stripped of my wet clothes, wrapped in a blanket, and sat down to wait for breakfast. Hot bullion out of a package restored some life, a fried egg sandwich even more. Leah was a heroine to stand in that noisy jumping galley, seasick as she was, to get it for me. I told her so.

"I need you," she explained, "to get us back to land and off this fucking boat. Never, you hear, never, are you getting me on the sea again."

"I tried to get you and Mary to stay home," I reminded her, "you could be in Paris now wondering how we got on with our expedition."

"I thought you needed a keeper," she told me.

Couldn't argue with that. We sat together as the weary day wore on, occasionally braving the elements in the pilothouse to check the radar and the engine instruments. Mike appeared briefly, looked out of the cabin windows at the maelstrom surrounding us and went back to his cabin. I didn't blame him. When our destination finally showed up on the radar I got dressed more formally for the required interview with customs. I stationed Leah to guard the doors until we had been cleared, as there is a rather daunting fine to pay if anyone leaves the ship before customs says it's OK.

I moved us to the visitor's dock to dine on land. I for one wasn't ready to tackle the canal system without a lot of rest. My crew went further than this. All but Leah left after dinner by taxi for the airport to fly back to Paris. The boat was cold and damp, still too wet to start the generator. Leah in her thickest flannel outfit slept with me, so we were quite warm and cozy. She was very warm and cuddly, so I had some difficulty thinking of her as a sister. But I was too tired anyway. Natasha and Mikel I could understand, but Mike's desertion rankled. Here I was making him rich, taking him on all sorts of exciting adventures, letting him play with a nuclear bomb, and when the going got tough he ran out on me.

In the morning I got supplies from the nearest hardware stores to patch the Celestine up for a run back home. I nailed a plastic tarp over the roof, lapped down over the top of the windows. Tubes and tubes of caulking went into the seams of the inexpertly applied plywood. A flameless alcohol heater dried the inside so the generator would run again. The following day we set out on a leisurely cruise through the French countryside, stopping where we liked, eating in cheap cafes. Leah admitted that this sort of boating she could get used to. I was somehow afraid to say that I'd begun to feel that with Leah I could get used to anything. The weather was cold, with rain sometimes but after what we'd been through it was nothing. The water trickled steadily into the engine room, but with the boat not rolling it too was harmless. I was really sorry when we stood watching the Celestine rumbling out of the water on the boatyard rails for the second refit in a month.

My crew was nicely settled into the Mela Corporation's rented villa just outside Paris. Joe had a computer with radio connection to Terreau in our office downtown. He had become the center of a whole new division at Terreau, busy with commercial designs of the finder and new applications. They would soon be working off the hundred million and sending us new ten percents. Mikel and Natasha had no part in this, so were making contacts to sell freelance nature and recreation articles for French and American magazines. They had the start of a promising new career going. Mike was ashamed of himself, full of abject apologies, excused himself on the grounds the cold and the motion of the boat were just too much for him. Of course I accepted, but we were never real friends afterwards.

I had not expected any further mention of our successful mission, figuring everyone involved wanted to pretend the whole thing never happened. I was wrong again. Two days after I got back a messenger delivered a package as we were digesting breakfast. In it were separate envelopes for each of us. I opened mine, and in surprise announced. "Well I'm damned, Terreau has invited us to a formal dinner in our honor, black tie, evening . . ."

A sort of whooshing sound interrupted me, followed by a soft implosion as the air rushed in to fill the vacuum left by three rapidly departing bodies. An instant later came the sound of car doors slamming, followed by the squeal of tires of a Citroen taking off in hot pursuit of something. As the dust settled and the building stopped rocking Joe remarked thoughtfully "I believe the girls have gone shopping for evening dresses."

I must say the Mela Corporation cleaned up nicely, We gathered outside the ballroom for dinner and speeches making a fine show. Leah and Mary were spectacular in marginally decent gowns, Natasha had gone high-fashion-slinky to great effect. Joe appeared with a very French woman, if you know what I mean, on his arm. Big liquid eyes, a gown obviously not only made for her but also designed for her, that indefinable air of the clothes only being temporary. It took me a moment to recognize her as M. Lemaire's secretary. The males were smart but not gaudy in hurriedly purchased evening suits, not identical as some favored soft fronts, some hard. Joe introduced his partner as "You all know Celestine," which explained something I had wondered about. William had a partner from Terreau's legal department, not someone I would have chosen but he seemed pleased with her. He acted distracted, worried, not into the spirit of the affair. I asked him why. "Oh," he said, "it's a problem that's bothering me. Don't worry about it now, we'll discuss it tomorrow." So I put it out of my mind to enjoy the evening.

Cocktails and canapés started us off in the assembly room leading to the ballroom. We were introduced to Terreau management and some rather distinguished members of the government, including an air force general who shook my hand very vigorously while murmuring "Merci, merci, my career. We can rely on your continued discretion?" I assured him we were all doing our best to forget the whole thing completely, though some of us would have nightmares about it for the rest of our lives. To this day I wake up in the middle of the night reliving the moment when I dropped the boat anchor on The Object.

I stuck to white wine in anticipation of the dinner. Indeed it was magnificent, course after course each with it's own wine. Head table of course. The girls glowed. When it was all finished and cleared away we got coffee, brandy, and the speeches. They could of course hardly say they were honoring us for saving their asses by recovering a nuclear bomb they had carelessly dropped in a friendly neighbor's principal port. Instead we had 'performed a hazardous and delicate mission with the utmost valor and discretion for Terreau CSF and Le Republique.' The girls got special mention for their part. Leah practically purred. "Almost worth that ghastly ride back" she muttered. Each of the crew of the Belle Celestine got a plaque to hang in their offices complete with enameled tricoleur memorializing the affair. I wasn't sure I wanted to be reminded of it, but didn't say so. I got a special presentation in a fancy box that they urged me to open right away. It contained a bottle of Chivas Regal. I stood to reply to all this, mentioned that we could not have performed the unspecified task without the support of our many Terreau colleagues, but especially the tireless efforts of M. Lemaire. I mentioned that Natasha and Mikel had made a vital contribution, Mary and Leah had provided essential logistic support, and of course Dr Jenkins' enormous professional skill and dedication made the whole mission possible. Mike and I, I said, had provided transportation. I sat down to applause and Leah kissed me.

The Chairman of the board of Terreau then stood up to make an unscheduled speech. He said he wanted to correct the modest impression I had given, which I didn't think I had. He reminded them that I had been the leader of the enterprise providing the direction and motivation to continue with it in the teeth of what he called 'difficulties extreme.' I stood up to say the bottle of

Chivas was ample recompense for the difficulties surmounted, and that I would gladly undertake any other such missions for Terreau for the same compensation.

The tables were cleared back to open the dance floor, a live orchestra filed in, and those with the energy got up to show off their gowns. Leah insisted I dance with several Important Wives as well as herself. She danced with several Important Husbands and several other eager Frenchmen. In the course of the evening, so she claimed, she had several interesting propositions and one offer of marriage from a Very Rich Person. As he was easily old enough to be her father she reluctantly refused. How much of this was true and how much teasing me I never discovered.

The evening ended about two a.m. The distinguished Dr Jenkins vanished, the rest of us went home in a Terreau limo. A very pleasant night out, very kind of Terreau. When we got in I opened the Chivas to offer as a nightcap. "By the way," I asked William, "what was worrying you earlier?"

"I talked to Blake in LA earlier. He's just been served with papers. SQV is suing us for return of stolen industrial secrets and disgorgement of all monies derived from their sale or use."

We finished the Chivas.

Chapter 16

The morning found us in a formal board meeting of the Mela Corporation, Mary and Leah there to take real minutes. All those present had a suitably grave expression, some also clutching coffee trying to remember where they were. We, especially Mary, had enjoyed the dinner and reception. She had fooled us by remaining vertical and coherent all night, concealing the fact she was full to the brim of Terreau CSF hospitality and gratitude. Mike told us an interesting anecdote about the interaction late in the evening between Mary and a member of the US consular staff. Mary gave him a look of pure hatred.

The chairman, namely me, called the meeting to order.

"OK, let's get down to business. There is a quorum of the board present, Blake only absent. You all know why we're here. We expected SQV to do something like this, it should be no surprise. If we'd been cleverer about publishing that recording things might have been different, and William might not have been assaulted, but that's all in the past. Now we know SQV and maybe the FBI will play dirty so we have to plan a campaign as if our lives and checking accounts depended on it. William and I meet later today with Monsieur 'call me Charles' Lemaire to keep him informed."

"Wow, did he really say that?" Leah asked, "you must be in favor with Terreau. That's equivalent to being given a key to the executive washroom."

"He thinks we've kept him out of a penal colony, he should be grateful. We need to develop a broad plan of attack. We know they've no claim to the Finder, don't see how they can establish one, but they wouldn't have filed a suit unless they thought they could make some sort of case. For a start, we need to file counterclaims, delay the case, ask for a jury trial, everything possible to mess them up. William, should you go back to California to work on it?"

"Christ no," he said with feeling. "I'll hire a gang of shysters who are really good at this sort of stuff. One broken leg is enough for now."

"I don't think they'll go after you again, what would they gain? But I do understand your feelings. Go ahead, show them we'll fight. Joe is going to stay in Paris making us all rich, he'll have to come to LA for the trial if it gets to that, but he can stay here with Celestine and talk mathematics to Francois until then. Mike, what would you like to do?"

"I'd like to go home," he said wistfully, "but I don't think I will. Let me work on planning strategy. I've got a book, 'The Art of War' that has some really good ideas."

"Splendid, I've already followed part of Sun-Tzu's advice. I've been studying SQV on my new phone, downloading their annual report, looking at the stock market analysts. I think they have a weakness we may be able to use, I'll tell you about it later. Mary, when you feel better what do you want to do? There's nothing to stop you going home if you want."

"And leave Paris when I've got money to spend for the first time in my life? When I get invited to formal dinners with diplomats and rich people? I'll stay if you'll let me, with Mike. Unless I have to go in that boat again."

I forced myself to ask the next question. "Leah, you're a free agent. We need you as the company secretary and official translator, but it's up to you."

"I said you need a keeper, you lunatic, of course I'm going to stay. I'll even go in the boat. If it stays in the canals."

The board of directors then formally instructed the corporation attorney to proceed with a vigorous defense and countersuit, and resolved to continue to do business from our Paris office sine die.

Months passed before we had a court date. We each spent it in our own way. Mikel and Natasha went adventuring in places nobody had ever heard of, including being among the survivors of an ill-conceived ride down an ice-filled Siberian river. Mary dived into the Paris scene, pulling Mike in after her. Joe divided his time between the new sonar devices division of Terreau and the charming Celestine. Leah and I worked on my new vision for the Mela Corporation and made some scenic tours of Europe, including a memorable ride on the new Orient Express. Still on a sisterly basis that I was afraid to try to alter.

As the trial date neared we went on the offensive per Mike's war plan, starting with doing everything we could to prejudice the jury. We had two weapons. One was on a disc in my office safe, the other unfortunately was in a safe deposit box in Santa Monica. We already knew how anxious SQV was to get hold of the recording of the FBI making fools of themselves, so flying in and picking the disc up might well be tantamount to suicide. I had carefully set up the box so only I personally could access it. This didn't seem as clever a move now as it had when I did it.

The other weapon was the article Natasha had written for Geographica. Mike had studied the magazines in the field to come up with one that had a wide popular circulation but was considered sound by the profession. 'Archeology Today' was his choice. I called the editor in New York at four in the morning Paris time. After the preliminaries I got down to planning his future.

"Yes, what I'm calling about is an article which you may want to do a special issue on. This is something completely new, will significantly change underwater archeology. I'm offering it to you exclusively so long as it issues on the date I want."

Naturally he was a little skeptical. "Look in your email," I told him, "there's a sample illustration from the article in it. Yes, I'll hold."

He had a whole different attitude when he came back on. Before I gave him any more though I got an undertaking of complete confidentiality until the magazine actually reached the bookstores. No advance publicity beyond a promise of something interesting coming, nothing about underwater. He wanted the author to come to his office so they could go over the text and photo selection together. I told him he'd have to come to Paris for it. This stuck until I said I'd pay.

Two days later he got the whole treatment including a playthrough of our best recordings on a Finder display in Joe's laboratory at Terreau, Joe's life story, a visit to the partly dismantled Belle Celestine, long sessions with Natasha and Mikel making the article long enough for a whole special issue. Enough to get him so excited he wanted to advance the issue date. Absolutely not, we told him, otherwise no article.

Mike and I couldn't think of any safe way to get the disc in Santa Monica. Leah's solution, "Don't go!" was touching but not helpful. We worked out a very risky and uncertain plan. My crew again had a unanimous opinion of the enterprise. "You're out of your mind."

"This time," I informed them, "I'm going alone. It's dangerous and one can slip about easier than two."

I got another unanimous opinion. "Let you go out in the big world by yourself? No way." Leah was more explicit. "You're not going anywhere without a keeper. Besides, you have exciting adventures."

We compromised. Leah would come as far as Vancouver BC and maintain a base while I made the raid into hostile territory to get that recording. "You'll like Vancouver," I told her, "and we'll take a ride to Victoria to see the Butchart gardens illuminated."

"I don't know about that," she said, "you have to go by boat and I don't trust you around boats any more."

Air France to Montreal naturally required a stopover to try the food, just for a comparison with Paris. Not bad, perhaps in some ways better. Then Air Canada to Vancouver and the Four Seasons hotel. I was used by this time to the open amazement of hotel clerks when I asked for separate rooms for my colleague and myself. They always gave us adjoining ones. Once settled in and rested we equipped ourselves with overnight bags and took the ferry to Victoria, ostensibly for a tour of Butchart Gardens. Instead I kissed Leah farewell, not quite brotherly, to catch the antique ferry to Seattle. I felt glad to leave her in the safety of Vancouver so I could travel light to Santa Monica.

The US customs is usually a formality. "Citizenship? Where do you live? Are you taking anything back?" I got something extra. "Some identification please."

I tried not to stiffen up, look like I hadn't a care. The inspector glanced at my driver's license and waved me on through. I watched to see if he asked anyone else for ID. Nobody. Well, I never thought this was going to be easy. I took a cab, had him let me off within walking distance of what I thought would be a way to get to LA that nobody would dream I would use. The evening Amtrak. I was sure nobody had followed me as I walked into the station, so hoped 'they' were waiting hopefully for me at SeaTac airport. Whoever 'they' might be. If the US Customs were looking out for me the FBI had to be at the bottom of it.

The train ride wasn't as bad as I expected, though I wouldn't say it compared favorably with the Orient Express. Different class of food for one thing. Instead of riding to the end at LA Union Station, I dropped quietly off the train at Santa Barbara. An hour's drive up the coast from LA in case you've never been there. I had to get a cab again, which leaves a trail, but after having him drive me round for a while got out in the middle of a residential block. I walked one block to the used car lot I'd spotted to get wheels for the next phase of the raid.

A gray Chevy of some anonymous middle-size model suited me perfectly, inconspicuous to the point of invisibility. A long way from new, but not old enough to be noticeable. I dickered for it cash, made out the registration in my own name to match my license in case I got stopped for some trivial traffic infraction, and drove off for the east with the salesman's careful directions for finding the Casitas Pass road inland. Once out of sight I turned back to the coast road for a relaxing scenic ride to Santa Monica and my safe deposit box. After suitable formalities I got the precious disc, rushed to a local computer store for three copies, and rushed back to put the original safely into the bank's vault again. So far I hadn't spotted anyone following me, even better I hadn't had my leg broken and the disc stolen. Maybe all my precautions, sudden turns, tours round the block looking for a following car, were unnecessary. This all seemed too easy.

I mailed one disc to myself at the Four Seasons, the other to Leah. The third I kept in my pocket to have something to hand over if I did get assaulted. I left the Chevy with the keys in it in the long-term parking at LAX to be stolen, to take the first plane going in the general direction of Canada. This landed me back in Seattle, tired, needing a shower, and very pleased with myself. There were no more planes to Vancouver for that day so I took a motel room for the night. I spent the evening looking for a gift for Leah, stuck all this time waiting for the warrior's return. As it had turned out she could just have well have come, no danger at all that I could see. The jewelry stores were a disappointment after Paris, mostly 14kt gold that is actually over 60% base metal by volume. 18kt they didn't seem to have heard of. Eventually I found a platinum heart locket on a chain, set with some nice diamonds, brought out of the vault when the store proprietor decided I really wanted to spend some money. He seemed surprised when my credit card went straight through, but so long as the amount is under ten thousand they don't usually ask to speak to me. I put the little velvet box in my pocket to give Leah as soon as I saw her. She wanted diamonds, these would make a good start.

Next morning early I caught Alaska Air to Vancouver. Still no sign of the FBI or thugs from SQV. I got to the hotel by midday, feeling inordinately pleased with myself. I stopped to pick up my mail at the front desk, though my letter to myself couldn't have got here yet. The clerk handed me an envelope with my name in block letters but nothing else on it. Hand delivered obviously. Odd, I didn't know anyone in Vancouver and the writing wasn't Leah's. There was a plain card inside with block capitals printed on it. My whole world collapsed down to this message:

FOR EVERY ONE OF THOSE RECORDINGS YOU SEND OUT WE SEND YOU A PIECE OF YOUR GIRLFRIEND.

And I thought I'd been so clever.

Chapter 17

"Call the police," I yelled at the desk clerk, "she's been kidnapped."

A brief reluctance to lowering the tone of the hotel by having police in the lobby lost out to the need to keep me quiet. The Vancouver police came, took details, asked questions, took the note away for forensics, but didn't have much constructive to offer. The housekeeping staff confirmed Leah's bed had not been slept in last night, otherwise nobody had seen her or knew when she went out. In the middle of this I stamped up and down the lobby swearing at my own foolishness, off having fun while they stole Leah. I was only too familiar with the statistics of kidnapping. The vast majority of victims are dead and the bodies hidden before the ransom note even goes out.

Logically, I should mourn my poor Leah but go ahead with our plans so as not to let all the others down. Practically the idea of getting some grisly bundle in the mail to prove Leah had been terribly hurt prevented me from imagining sending those recordings off. She might still be alive, though it didn't matter to them what they did if I went ahead, so they had no reason to keep her. If they wanted to hurt me even more they could keep what they needed in the freezer. When that idea occurred to me I got the shakes, had to sit down with my head between my knees for a minute. What could I do? The resources marshaled against us were too much. I called Mike in Paris to share the bad news.

"What can I do? How can I get her back? Think of something . . . "

"Calm down a minute," he broke in, " let me think."

I resisted the temptation to bang the telephone on the counter. He came back on.

"Do you really think the FBI is involved?"

I had to think about that. The clue I thought lay in that brief delay at Seattle customs. "Yes, don't know if they actually did the kidnapping but I'm sure they had a hand in it."

"Then let's make them help get her back," he said.

When I was, as he put it, through yelping, he explained. Nothing reasonable would work, so he laid out a most unreasonable plan for me. He offered to hop a plane to help but I told him stay put, this is risky enough for one.

"And brief William," I told him, " so if there are legal consequences he can at least find me a lawyer."

By a considerable amount of transferring from one directory assistance to another I got connected to the FBI office in LA. "Let me speak to agent Jones, right now."

"Agent Jones is not in the office at the moment, some other agent can help you."

"Oh no they can't, this concerns Jones and if I don't speak to him very soon he's going to regret it very much."

The FBI took umbrage. "I'm sure making threats is not going to help, sir, anybody here can help you if you have a legitimate problem."

"I have a kidnapping which agent Jones had better get involved in. Take my number, get in touch with him, have him call me. He'll know my name."

Ten stamping, cursing, minutes I waited in my hotel room for the call. The phone beeped. "Jones!" I yelled at it.

"This is agent Jones. I don't think there's anything you and I have to talk about."

"Oh, isn't there," I grated. "Try this for size. If I don't call Paris by midday tomorrow there's going to be a press conference for all the worlds news agencies, including TASS and the People's Republic of China. They are going to see a 3-D film of an American nuclear submarine out of San Diego at cruising speed under water, complete with depth, time, and distance markers. You are going to be quoted as giving permission for its release. By name, with your office telephone number. Now do we have something to talk about?"

"You can't do that, that's . . . that's treason." I had him yelling now.

"And kidnapping is a federal crime, so we can trade." Not that I cared any more, I wanted Leah back if she was still alive. And I didn't care what I had to do to get her.

"I don't know anything about a kidnapping, what can I do?" Jones, trying to sound reasonable.

"Then I'll let them go ahead with the press conference. Expect to be the center of attention by tomorrow morning."

"What do you want from me?" He wailed.

"I want Leah returned alive and well. Soon. Start work and call me back. Ten minutes should be plenty of time. Remember it's already one in the morning in Paris."

I switched the phone off without waiting for a reply. Don't give him time to think, keep the pressure on.

I got room service to send up some coffee and a brandy while I waited. Just one drink, resist the temptation to get blind drunk. Fifteen minutes went by before the telephone beeped again. "Well," I said to it.

"They won't give her up, they say it's my problem. But I think I know where she is." A nice subdued worried Jones, just what I needed.

"I want to know where Leah is, I want you personally with your gun, I want us to go get her back. If she's alive maybe you come out of it alive. If she's not you don't."

"I can't do that!"

"It's two a.m. in Paris. I'll need to call soon."

He squirmed about on the hook but I kept pushing, reminding him of the damage the movie would do and the chances he would take all the blame for it. I announced the time in Paris in the spaces in the conversation to keep him on his toes. In the end he agreed, of course. Poor Leah, This was the best I could do. If she was dead I had every intention of shooting Jones. Except I didn't have a gun.

"Where is she?"

"In a house east of Seattle. I have the address, never been there so I don't know the tactical situation." Jones talking like the FBI.

"Right, I'll meet the first plane at SeaTac from LAX in the morning. You come alone, no help, no backup. This is a private war, keep the FBI out of it. Remember, I'll change the press conference to happen the day after tomorrow if I don't call, so you better keep me healthy and talking."

I checked us both out of the hotel, packed Leah's bags with mine. Her scent made me cry. An expensive cab ride to the border, another to the nearest Hertz office. I rented a good powerful four-door car, white to be reasonably inconspicuous. Then a long drive to the same fucking motel I'd just left in Seattle. I had to get a grip on myself driving to keep to the prevailing speed, not be obviously wild. All the way I talked to myself, reproaching myself for letting this happen. I thought suddenly of another kidnapped person, Judy the Geographica editor. Nothing had been heard of her again. She must have relatives, a lover, people who had felt just as I did without even knowing why it had happened. All the times I had treated Leah like a favorite sister, when we might have been lovers. Don't rush, that's the ridiculous idea I'd had. There's always a rush, tomorrow is too dangerous to defer things to.

The desk clerk asked if I felt quite well as I checked in. When I looked in the mirror I could see what he meant. Red rimmed eyes, and a new expression I didn't know I had. As if I were about to snarl. That idea got me back to the front desk with a difficult problem.

"I need to buy a gun, hand gun," I told him. "And money's no object. Where do you suggest I go?"

No false indignation about this lad. "How much money and what sort of gun?"

"Whatever it takes, and a small automatic, twenty-five or similar. With some shells."

"Just step in the office a moment." He produced a very nice little American-made automatic and half a box of shells. "What is this worth?"

I took it, pulled back the action to eject a shell, examined it. "Very good, just what I need. The retail on this is what, two or three hundred?"

"Retail," he said. "For someone not in a hurry."

"I think it's worth a thousand in a hurry. Not more, I can go touring the bars and do better than that."

"Cash?"

"Half will have to be a check unless you have a teller machine?"

"Check will do, I know your credit card number and the limit on it. Your check is good. For half."

I went to bed cuddling that gun. I didn't expect to sleep but the alarm woke me at seven in time to get dressed to go to meet the plane I hoped Jones would be on. The gun made a barely noticeable bulge in my back pocket. I was early at the airport, so forced myself to eat breakfast. I couldn't remember when I last ate. Jones appeared dressed in the regulation suit, unmistakably an FBI agent standard model. He carried an overnight bag.

"Got your gun?" I asked. He nodded. We walked to the short term parking to get the car. "Right, you drive to this house where Leah had better be for both our sakes. Go past and park so we can have a look at it."

"Better let me lead," he suggested, "I've got the training for it."

"OK. Wait, stop here. There's a hardware store, I want something."

I shot into the store to buy a two-foot long wrecking bar, an excellent quiet weapon. Jones wanted to know what I wanted with that, so I explained that since I didn't have a gun because I'd just come from Canada I needed something in my hand. An ace up the sleeve is worth any amount of skill.

Jones drove, I watched the traffic behind for tails. He swore he had come alone without telling anyone where he was going. I believed him of course. I kept checking. Well out in the country he pointed to a small run-down two-story house, in need of paint and roof work. We stopped well past it then strolled back to reconnoiter. Nothing showed, no sign of life. Jones wanted to watch for a day to observe the routine so he could plan an approach. Yeah, right.

"Find a stone to throw. When I wave throw it hard at the front door then duck behind the hedge." He started to argue. Suddenly all my rage and frustration boiled over. I snarled at him "Do what I tell you, never mind wasting time with nonsense. Get a rock to knock on the front door." I pulled the wrecking bar out of my pants leg where it had been hanging and waved it. "Now."

He grubbed around and found a brick, just the thing. I walked up the weedy path and stood flat against the wall at the handle side of the front door, then waved to Jones. The brick hit with a loud whump. The door opened and a short olive skinned man peered out. He was just a shade slow seeing me beside him. The heavy end of the wrecking bar made a very satisfying crunch on his skull.

Jones ran up with his small cannon in his hand. "Christ, you've killed him," he whispered. I nodded proudly. A voice called from inside somewhere. "Mario?" Then something in Spanish. Jones was up the corridor like a cat. The caller opened a door to find himself facing Jones' gun. I held up my trusty weapon.

"Where's the girl?" I shouted at him.

Some nonsense about no comprend, what girl. "Shoot his balls off, see if he remembers then," I told Jones.

"Upstairs, upstairs, no shoot."

"Lead the way, carefully if you want to stay whole."

He walked slowly and reluctantly up the stairs with Jones' gun poking in his back. "There," he pointed to a door with sweat running down his face, "in there."

"You, open the door first," Jones commanded.

Inside the room the only furniture was a single bed against the wall in one corner. The room smelled bad. On the bed bundled up in a blanket lay a very still figure.

Chapter 18

"You've killed her," I shouted at our captive.

"No, no," he pantomimed giving an injection, "she sleeps, just sleeps."

I knelt down by the bed to lift the blanket away from her face. She had a black eye and a black and yellow bruise on her cheek. Her face felt warm and as I bent over to kiss her she sighed without moving. Alive! My other self took over. The gun appeared in my hand by some sort of reflex. "You hurt her," I snarled. I pulled the trigger to send him crumpling to the floor.

"What the hell did you do that for," Jones asked, stooping over my second victim. Unnecessarily, he was quite dead. The wrecking bar, if you should ever decide to go to the extreme to show you dislike someone, is much more satisfactory than shooting. Both however have the same desirable result of satisfying that dark thing lurking in our reptilian brain ready to defend our mate and territory with teeth and claws.

I took two quick steps to press my gun against Jones' skull. "Now give me your gun, very carefully butt first." I put my little one away. His didn't fit my pockets.

He pulled himself up to his full height. "Well, go ahead. Shoot me if you must."

"Not right now," I told him, "I need you. Go get the car, back it up to the door and open the back doors. On your way drag that thing in the doorway inside the house. And don't think of taking off, nothing has changed in Paris."

While he fetched the car I piled up everything burnable I could find in the kitchen with a sprinkling of cooking oil over my bonfire. I wrapped Leah in all the bedclothes to carry her down the stairs into the car. We went down with Jones on the feet while I carried the heavy end. I sat her upright with the seatbelt tight to hold her. I thought she would breath easier sitting up. She didn't stir through the whole careful maneuver.

"Right," I told Jones, "get ready to drive to a hospital while I set fire to the house."

"Wait a minute," he insisted, "search the rest of the house first. There might be someone else hiding."

Good point. Nothing downstairs. Upstairs there were three doors we hadn't opened. Each one we approached like it might have someone hiding behind it. One disclosed a dirty old-fashioned bathroom, one an empty bedroom, just dust. When we slammed the last door open we saw the duplicate of the one where Leah had been. This one smelled much worse. On the bed lay another blanket wrapped body. The head showed on this one, tight drawn like a death mask. "It's a corpse," I whispered, "what are we going to do with it?"

Jones walked reluctantly over to the bed to touch the thing's cheek. "It's alive, warm anyway."

We wrapped it up in blankets, filthy as it was, to put into the car opposite Leah who hadn't moved. Things were seeping through both sets of wrappings, to the detriment of Hertz's upholstery. I didn't worry about it. I made a quick run into the house to start the bonfire with a piece of paper towel lit on the stove. Back in the car with a splendid funeral pyre well underway in the kitchen I pressed 'hospitals' on the GPS menu screen. The damned thing gave me a list of 69 hospitals with no clue as to which had an emergency room. "Hitting it won't help," Jones advised. "Helps me," I replied. Eventually I settled on Northwest. I gave directions from the screen while he concentrated on getting us there with dispatch without exciting the local police.

We pulled up to the emergency room doors. In a few minutes both our rescuees were safely in the hands of doctors and nurses. After a few minutes fussing a harassed intern suggested we get a cup of something hot and sweet and pull ourselves together. Then stop by the business office. And keep out of his way. "I'll have to make a police report on this," he added. Agent Jones produced his wallet with photo ID and a badge. "No need, I'm from the FBI, we already know about it." This apparently satisfied the requirements. We were shooed out in the direction of the cafeteria.

"Just a minute," I told Jones, "is it safe to leave Leah unprotected? Do we need to guard her?"

"I don't think so, nobody alive knows we've got her yet. Later maybe. You need to sit quietly and calm yourself right now. May I have my gun back?"

"Later maybe." With which he had to be satisfied.

A cup of coffee didn't help me a lot, so we went to the business office. I told them I was responsible for the two emergency patients we'd just brought in. I gave them my credit card, told them we wanted private rooms for each when they came out of emergency. I didn't let myself think about it as 'if.' I told them Leah's name, but claimed I knew nothing about the other. Just as I turned away from the counter to go harass the emergency room again it came to me.

"Wait though, I know who it might be. I didn't recognize her, but the hair color is right. Call Geographica magazine, I think it may be their editor who got kidnapped months ago. She must have relatives who think she's dead." I rounded on Jones, putting my hand in my pocket where my little gun lay. "You, you must have known it was her."

"No, no, I had no idea," he stepped back away from me, he'd seen that look on my face before, "I swear, I had no idea. I've never seen her, don't know anything about it. Don't go crazy, don't start shooting in the hospital."

The woman on the counter asked loudly "Shall I call the police?"

Jones produced his ID again. "FBI ma'am, no need. Everything is under control."

"Well go and be under control somewhere else, not in the hospital."

We went back to emergency. I asked the nurse on the desk for news. She sent for the intern.

"They have both had massive overdoses of some drug. We're doing blood tests to see what it is before we can treat them. One of them is also suffering from dehydration and starvation. Plus she's got bedsores and some other lesions. Some septicemia. The other has some severe bruises, no other physical damage I could find. I think she'll come out of it, but we need to know what they've been given before we make a prediction for how they'll be. The other . . . " I interrupted, "I think her name's

Judy." He nodded, "She is very weak, we have her on life support. I am concerned about brain damage."

"What are you doing for Leah?"

"Right now we've cleaned her up, put in an IV with electrolytes, connected a monitor for heart action. We have to watch for a sudden collapse of vital functions. That's all we can do until the blood tests come back."

That's Leah he's talking about, his words trickling into me like ice. Sudden collapse of vital function. I turned to look at agent Jones. "I'm sorry, I'm sorry, I didn't know all this would happen," he moaned, "it all got away from us. SQV is desperate to get hold of Jenkin's invention."

I turned back to the intern. "I want to send a couple of armed guards for these poor girls. Can that be arranged?"

"Not in emergency it can't. They can stay outside. When we move the patients to rooms they can have guards outside the door."

I led agent Jones outside to have a talk. "Now I've got a problem. I can't let you loose, but I don't need you any more. If I let you go back to LA you'll get into mischief of some sort. I want you where I can see you until Leah is on a plane to Paris. Non stop. Then there's Judy, if she lives. The easy way is to shoot you and get it over with, but I'm not mad enough at you to do it. What do you suggest?"

"If I undertake not to do anything more will that do?" he said hopefully.

"Joking aside," I went on, "the only thing I can think of is to take your ID and keep your gun. I can get a couple of Pinkerton men to baby-sit you until I'm ready."

"I can't give up my ID."

"It's better than being dead," I pointed out.

We compromised, with the press conference in Paris still hanging over his head. I got the badge and gun, he got to stay loose at the motel.

Pinkerton seemed quite used to providing bodyguards. One for each girl twenty-four hours a day. With that set up I had time to call Paris to bring the rest of the company up to date on life on the wild side. I also remembered to ask them to send my credit card company a substantial payment. I took Jones to the motel, went back to wait for news on Leah. It was a long long night.

First thing in the morning Leah had recovered enough to move to a private room. She still slept soundly but, so they said, was successfully metabolizing the drug. The doctor in charge however still had reservations about what long term effects there might be. Judy had not responded so well. She was listed as critical in intensive care. I managed to get in to visit Leah. Her eye looked worse, but the bruise on her cheek had faded a little. I fitted the present I'd bought her very carefully round her neck so if she did wake she'd know someone loved her. I sat beside her on the hard guest chair with my eyes closed to rest them for a moment. Next thing I knew a nurse shook me, told me I had to leave now while they looked after her.

Leah did come round, a bit at a time. At first she didn't recognize me. Then she sobbed and sobbed remembering something she wouldn't talk about. She found the diamond heart when I wasn't there, acted like a little child over it, still pretty confused about where she was. The doctor didn't want her to travel, I wanted her back in Paris. I got my way by sending for a nurse to come from Paris to look after her on the flight back, first class by British Air to London then Air France to Paris. Every step of the way until the plane doors closed a stalwart Pinkerton man walked on each side of her. Agent Jones got back his ID and gun at the loading ramp, unloaded of course. We both thought he was lucky to be alive.

Judy did have relatives, who turned up to take over. I avoided, by being in Paris, tedious discussions of how she came to be in a Seattle hospital critical care unit when last seen in New York. They'll have to know all about it sometime, but not right now. For one thing there were two incinerated corpses, the presumed victims of a business dispute over drugs, from which I wished to disassociate myself. She would, I understood, recover physically, eventually, but what her mental condition would be only time would tell.

Leah didn't want to go into hospital in Paris, so she came back to the Mela Corporation villa. I kept the nurse until Leah got well enough to insist she wasn't a fucking child and for christ sake could bloody well go to the bathroom by herself. We judged from this she had recovered. I hired full time security guards for the house and office.

She wears the diamond heart constantly. It symbolizes for her our new relationship, and is also by way of being the equivalent of a security blanket. She certainly goes to sleep fingering it. The Belle Celestine, formerly Mela Mermaid, formerly Wilmington Steam Navigation Company Number 16, completed her third refit since I bought her. Two new sections of planking now kept the water out, even, the yard assured me, if it should be maximally unquiet. The new pilothouse, with mahogany, sported all the computerized navigation equipment anyone could wish for. The salon and cabins lost their utilitarian air to an interior decorator of indeterminate sex but a strong sense of style. Leah and I spent our honeymoon in her.

Leah not only got her diamonds, she became a collector, on first name terms with the staff the most exclusive jeweler in Paris.

In case you have forgotten, this ghastly adventure succeeded in its primary purpose. We now had the recording of the FBI insulting Joe and trying to threaten us into giving the Finder to SQV. We could get back on track to get as much advantage as we could for the trial. And I owed someone a payback for mistreating Leah and Judy. I had set part of this payback quietly gestating in obscure offices in Los Angeles. A little surprise for SQV, one I had kept strictly between Joe, William, and myself. Of course, it depended on our prevailing in the suit by SQV.

Chapter 19

According to William, and the law firm engaged to support him, the recording couldn't be used in the trial, 'inadmissible' for reasons I don't pretend to understand. Instead we mailed copies to the NAACP, the NY Times, the LA Times, and the National Enquirer. Each had a cover letter carefully tailored to their individual aims and taste, and to their widely different reaction times. We tried to arrange for the two newspapers to publish first, then the Enquirer and then any reaction by the NAACP about a day later, all to happen a few days before the trial. The 'Archeology Today' article we timed to appear about a week before, figuring it would take longer to trickle into the consciousness of the average juror. The lawyers were not happy with this process, "It will look like a deliberate attempt to prejudice the jury" one of them told me. I congratulated him on his clear grasp of the situation.

The Mela Corporation made a grand re-entry to the USA at LAX off another luxurious Air France flight. We were met, by arrangement, by four Pinkerton men, uniformed and armed, to escort us until the trial. The press had been invited. The three ladies of the party had spent considerable time, and of course money, on the best Paris could provide in the way of casual travelling outfits. Celestine, who had now taken up Joe as a full time occupation, looked as usual very French. Mary tended to the flamboyant but with an air, Leah went for elegance. The female reporters present suddenly looked as if they had been dressed by the Salvation Army store. A respectable crowd gathered.

I was reluctantly persuaded by the reporters assembled to meet us to give an impromptu spur-of-the-moment interview that we had rehearsed for most of the flight over. "What," one of them wanted to know when I let them ask questions, "do you have to say about the FBI's denial that anyone called Jones had ever been assigned to the LA office?"

"I'm sure," I told them gravely, "that the FBI has good reason for their statement. You people have the resources to check it out, see if Jones has relatives or friends who remember his being there."

This happy thought resulted next day in a televised interview with Jones' tearful sister, discovered living in Encino. She wanted to know what had happened to her brother, who had vanished and was now being disclaimed by his employers.

Several questions were shouted at me about our need for armed bodyguards. I hoped this would come up. "Last time we were on this continent my wife was kidnapped in an attempt to prevent our mounting a defense in the SQV suit against Dr Jenkins and the Mela Corporation. She spent considerable time in hospital recovering from her injuries. Another lady who had the misfortune to be involved may never recover fully. Our company attorney, William Carson here, still limps from the broken leg he got when thieves ransacked his home to remove evidence in the case. Apparently the plaintiffs have so little merit to their claims that they have to resort to the methods of gangsters to win."

Any juror who didn't see the results next day on local TV or in his newspaper, real or electronic, would have to be blind and deaf.

I had a most delicate and difficult covert operation to start now we were back in LA, one that could truly get me into Federal court if it went wrong. You can stick up banks, murder your neighbors, or sell recreational chemicals on street corners, and only half-hearted attempts will be made to catch you at it. But just try stock market manipulation or insider trading and the SEC will have you in court disgorging your profits before you have time to book your flight to Buenos Aires. I was planning both those crimes. I started by giving my broker instructions that got him over to see me personally at the hotel where we were holed up.

"Now, tell me again what you want. I couldn't understand it over the phone." He meant he couldn't believe it.

"I want you to buy some stock for the Mela Corporation."

"Yes, I gathered that, but the amount, I didn't hear it right."

"I'll say it again. Buy a hundred million dollars worth of SQV stock if the price drops below twenty. That's about five million shares. It's been flat around thirty but the last few days have taken a couple of points off. Don't be in too much of a hurry, watch the momentum and get as good a price as you can. If I'm free I'll tell you when, but I may be busy."

"You haven't got a hundred million," he objected. "You have to settle in three days and I can't lend you that much. Or anywhere near."

"This is a cash deal, no margin. Here are three checks totaling the full amount. They are good but will take time to clear, so don't delay. And let's be clear, this is for Mela, not my personal account."

"How do you know the stock is going to drop like that?" he asked suspiciously.

"Let's just say I have a presentiment. If I'm wrong the trade won't get made so you'll be holding the money for me. It should look good in the money market fund." He wanted to discuss it but I reminded him the interest was around six thousand dollars a day so time really was money.

Investors, particularly those who manage mutual funds and pensions, are very nervous people. They also have a strong herd instinct. If some uncertainty gets rumored about a company's earnings prospects, or they have a lawsuit pending, or there's a hint of scandal about management, all the big houses tend to sell the stock at once, to the detriment of the price. I had, I hoped, created all those factors for SQV.

Trial morning Joe and I got to sit up front with William. Behind the rails the rest of the firm and their friends and relations formed our cheering section. Even Blake turned up, towing a girl who looked, beside our Parisienne products, as if he'd picked her up on a Hollywood street corner. She took one look at the competition and would have left if Blake hadn't grabbed her arm. "For crissake sit at the back," I hissed at him, "you're spoiling the image."

The whole morning wasted away in incomprehensible preliminaries. Lunch break didn't allow time for a real lunch so we trooped to the cafeteria. I could see on the faces of the various female clerks, legal assistants, stenographers, and trial attendees that JC Penny would never seem the same again.

Celestine particularly attracted goggle-eyed attention from the ladies, though Mary did well in the competition to fascinate males. Perhaps Leah's diamonds were unwise wear in the company of the assorted felons lunching with their equally disreputable attorneys. We had the Pinkerton men waiting outside for us, and the detectors on the doors prevented weapons entering the premises, still it was sort of scary.

The afternoon brought the start of jury selection. William wanted all black people who had seen the newspapers and TV coverage, especially any that had read the Archeology magazine article. The plaintiffs on the other hand wanted all white jurors who had never seen a newspaper and didn't own a TV. This created what you might call 'irreconcilable differences.' The process dragged on to a second day, then a third. Leah confided that night that the bench seat she'd been sitting on had now molded her permanently to a new and less desirable shape. I was able to demonstrate that it hadn't.

On the third day the judge pointed out to both attorneys that while the population of LA County was only about eight million adults, we didn't have time to interview each one of them. He also informed the plaintiff's attorney that the fact a prospective juror could read was not grounds for dismissing him for cause. As both sides had run out of wild cards the jury then sat.

The real business started next morning. We had not been able to imagine what evidence SQV could have for their claim. We soon found out. Earnest engineers came to the stand to swear they'd worked on the Finder while Joe followed other projects at SQV. Joe had the same security badge they did, so he could easily have taken notes of what they were doing. Joe bubbled quietly beside me, muttering things like "and I thought he was my friend." William did his best but couldn't find a crack to work on. By the evening he thought we might lose, all the good work in advance publicity now forgotten by the jury.

"But it's all lies, they can't just stand there and get away with that!" Welcome to the real world, Joe.

It was a silent and apprehensive Mela Corporation in court next day. SQV put on their centerpiece, Dr Brought, who had headed the operation where all this imaginary work was done.

His credentials, as presented by a smiling attorney, were impressive. Almost as good as Joe's. When he got through, including describing Joe as 'competent but not brilliant' it was William's turn. He did his best.

"Dr Brought, can you tell the court in layman's language what the operating principle of the device in questions is?"

Brought thought for a minute. "No," he said shaking his head.

"Why is that may I ask?"

"Because it's too complicated."

William thought he might be on to something here. "Well, try it the best you can so we may tell for ourselves."

Brought launched into techspeak. For a moment I thought I recognized some of the words he used. "Joe," I whispered, "that sounds like the title of your doctoral thesis."

Joe looked at me as if I was feeble-minded. "Well, of course . . . "

"Joe," I interrupted, "you may be a brilliant engineer but you're a complete idiot. Get out of here and find a computer, there must be one somewhere in this building. Print a copy of your thesis and get back here on the double."

We were interrupted by a peal from the judge. "Mr. Carson, can you not keep your client under control? I will not have private conversations going on during testimony."

"I beg your honor's pardon, may I have a moment to confer with my client?"

"A moment to keep him quiet," said the judge.

William stalked back to whisper to us "What the hell are you guys up to, upsetting the judge isn't going to help."

"Get going, Joe. William, keep this guy going for a few minutes. I think we can prove he's full of shit." I hoped.

William turned back to the witness, visibly trying to get himself back in the mood. After a pause he started to attack Brought.

"Now then, you say, if I understand you rightly, that the principle of the device is so arcane that only a select few highly educated people can understand it?"

"Well, I didn't put it quite like that, but in essence that is correct." Brought didn't see the catch to that but William did.

"How do you know, Dr Brought?" William asked in a conversational tone.

Brought looked puzzled. "I don't follow you," he admitted.

"How do you know what the principle of operation of the Finder is?" William asked in sweetly reasonable tones.

Brought opened his mouth to reply. He shut it again, realizing he had better think this through first. The SQV attorney jumped up to try and recover. "Oh, your honor, that's been answered. Dr Brought is a skilled engineer well able to understand the principle."

"Your honor, we don't dispute that he can understand it, I asked how he knew what it was."

"I think the witness had better answer the question," his honor decided. Before William could get back to the job Joe came clattering into the court waving a handful of papers.

"May I have a moment your honor?" William asked with deep respect. He got a grudging "I suppose so" for answer.

"Where's the good bit, Joe" I whispered. Joe riffled through to a page of mixed Greek and Hebrew characters in unlikely combination. "It's all here," he said. Could have fooled me. I folded the top and bottom of the page under and paperclipped it to a piece of paper off William's pad. I whispered instructions in William's ear. He stared at me then muttered to Joe, "You idiot, why didn't you tell us this months ago?" Joe looked confused. "I thought it was obvious," he said.

Chapter 20

William turned back to his victim.

"Now are we finally ready to proceed?" asked the judge.

"Yes your honor, thank you for your indulgence. Now, Dr Brought, let's leave that question you're having so much difficulty with for a moment and go on to something else. Would you be kind enough to glance at this document and tell the court what it is?"

Brought took the page out of Joe's thesis gingerly as if it might explode. He stared at it. "Hmm. Brilliant. A most economic statement of the key algorithm. This must have been stolen from my operation somehow."

"So you would say that was written by someone who fully grasped the principles involved?"

"Oh yes, yes indeed." He started to unfold the paper.

"Let's leave it like that for the moment," William said taking it back. He started to cross-examine again when the judge woke up. "Let me see that."

William handed it up to him. He unfolded the top to see the superscript. Plaintiff's attorney came rushing up to have a look too, but the judge handed it back to William with no change in his expression. "Proceed," he said.

"Now Dr Brought, are you ready to tell the court how you come to know the operating principle of the Mela Corporation's Finder device? Have you personally inspected it?"

"Well, um … er, no, not personally."

"Well then how?"

"A representative of the SQV Company inspected it."

William beamed at him. "Really, and this representative, was she a sufficiently skilled and experienced engineer that she could grasp the principle of operation by looking at it? If so, perhaps we need her on this witness stand."

Brought didn't seem to notice that the 'representative' had become 'she.' "Well, no, perhaps not."

139

Now William switched to indignation, "Come now Dr Brought, just tell the court how you know what the operating principle of the Finder is."

He tried to mutter an answer but the judge invited him to speak up. "I saw photos of the device and some drawings and computer programming charts."

"The property of Mela Corporation apparently stolen by a spy?" William thundered.

"Well, they were ours to start with," Brought shot back.

"Oh, Dr Brought, then perhaps you can explain to the court why you think a page out of Dr Jenkin's MIT doctoral dissertation from many years before he joined SQV was stolen from your operation?"

You could have heard a pin drop in the courtroom. The judge stared at Brought, the jury stared at Brought, the cheering sections behind the rails stared at Brought. The SQV attorney eventually found his voice. "May we see that document please your honor?"

Without waiting for the judge to answer William carefully smoothed out the page in question, collated it neatly back into the rest of the thesis, and handed it to him with a bow. William waited politely until he had finished looking it over. When the attorney went to hand it back William gravely told him to keep it, copies were freely available on the Internet, we could easily print another. He turned back to poor Dr Brought.

"Would you like me to repeat the question?"

Brought just stood there with his mouth opening and shutting. The attorney for the plaintiffs came out of a whispered conversation with the people in the pew behind him. "If it please your honor, may we have a recess to consider the possibility of an out-of-court settlement of this matter?"

"Mr. Carson?" asked the judge.

"Your honor, my client has been subject to suit and prevented from commercial exploitation of this valuable invention by what appears to be, not to put too fine a point on it, perjured testimony. Dr Jenkins has been insulted professionally and personally. I would like to hear the jury's verdict on this procedure. I would first though like to have the earlier witnesses back on the stand to repeat some of their testimony."

If I heard him correctly the plaintiff's attorney said "Growk." The judge announced "I think the court will recess for lunch. That will give the parties time to consider their positions." He then gave the jury the usual warning about not discussing the case or arriving at a conclusion until he instructed them. I think he wasted his breath.

A select few from each side met in an empty jury room. SQV had an interesting offer. Settle now for a license from SQV to use their invention. William left the negotiation to me.

"Very amusing I'm sure," I answered, "now let's get serious. You sit down and let the jury decide the suit in our favor. Then we want a billion dollars in damages in the suit we're going to file against SQV. And we are going to ask the State Attorney General's office to look into the testimony given in the case."

"You aren't serious!"

"Oh, aren't I. Just wait until the next jury hears from my wife about the kidnapping, and we produce that poor woman from Geographica. You'll be lucky not to get lynched."

"Really! Are you threatening us?"

I knew the answer to this old put-down. "Yes."

There didn't seem to be any grounds for a settlement here, and of course I didn't want one. We broke for a quick snack with the rest of our parties. William got kissed by all three of our ladies, to the evident envy of the male lunchers around us. Joe got called several different sorts of idiot. He kept asking in a dazed sort of a way "But what did I do?" Celestine kissed him anyway.

I wanted the proceeding to end before the markets closed, as I didn't think the overnight trading would accomplish our ends. That would be one-thirty California time, so we were already too late. Still, if we could finish this afternoon early I could start the campaign to mangle SQV's stock price.

The rest of the trial went very rapidly. The jurors were smiling at Joe, and I distinctly saw a lady juror wink at him. The judge in effect told them to go out and find for the defendants, the Mela Corporation. The foreman got an unintended laugh, to the judge's annoyance, by asking, "Do we have to go out?" They dutifully filed out to reappear in short order to find all the plaintiff's claims false.

I rushed out to find a quiet spot to start telephoning. I called my broker to tell him the case was over, and to tell all his friends that SQV now faced a huge damages suit plus possible criminal charges. I expected the news would spread through the stock market grapevine with the speed of light. Then I called the Business News channel. I gave them the scoop on SQV's humiliating defeat, the size and likely success of the Mela Corporation's countersuit for damages which would cripple SQV, and the fact that had they been caught in perjury. William had to get on the line to assure them of the truth of this item, as they thought it might well affect the value of SQV's stock. I thought they were probably right. And that completed a satisfactory day's work.

It took two limos to ferry us, Pinkerton included of course, to a discreet and very expensive French style restaurant in Huntington Beach. A most pleasant and convivial evening, what I remember of it. I think I enjoyed the food. Must have done.

Next morning at half-past six found me watching the business channel while clinging to a fizzy headache remedy. It wasn't a good day for SQV stockholders. On a normal day you'd hardly see their trades on the ticker, but this day they were prominent from the opening. It started well with an 'order imbalance.' Meaning a lot of people wanted to sell and nobody wanted to buy. The indicated opening, according to a shrill person reporting from the floor, looked like 22. Good, but not enough. I called my man to suggest he put in a bid for five million shares at 18. He said the way it looked we might do better than that, be patient. He had it right. When it did open it stabilized at 17. I thought five million shares would up the price, but instead of buying from the floor he managed to find a mutual that wanted out, so he got it for 17. Very nice, left almost fifteen million dollars in change. With the added bonus that the trade didn't show.

I went back to bed for an hour or two, feeling I'd already done more of a day's work than most people do in a lifetime.

I woke an hour later much refreshed to start my second day's work. I called our man at Merit/Hangtree to tell him the IPO, that's Initial Public Offering if you have been living in a cave since the nineteen-nineties, of the Mela Corporation was a GO. He already knew. William had called him the previous afternoon. One hundred million shares authorized, five million offered at 50. Out as soon as possible while the SQV affair still lingered in investor's minds. And that Archeology today article. I called William's room but he had gone already. He too had a busy day ahead, including filing suit against SQV.

Now I know a quarter of a billion dollars sounds like a lot of money, and of course compared with even quite extravagant housekeeping bills it is. I could dimly remember being very happy as a retired millionaire not very long ago in months, a whole lifetime ago it felt like. You have to understand that the bills to pay out of it came to a substantial sum, our friendly neighborhood investment bank in particular having lofty ideas as to the value of their services. In any case, even the whole amount wasn't close to what I needed. There is an old California saying to the effect that you have to look for gold where gold is. I needed to mine someone who could write billion dollar checks.

Leah appeared looking like I'd felt earlier before my bracing morning on the telephone. I called room service for coffee and croissants with a large orange juice for Leah. Then I started on my third day's work.

I dialed a Wisconsin number. It answered on the first buzz.

"Shakespeare-Grosvener. Good morning, how may I direct your call?"

"Mr. Grosvener please."

The operator found this laughable. "Mr. Grosvener is not available to take calls, can someone else help you?"

"Then connect me with someone who makes billion dollar decisions for him."

"Hold the line, I'll connect you with Mr. Hardcastle." Evidently, from her tone, the regular designee for dealing with crank calls.

"Hardcastle, what may I do for you?" In a distinct Harvard accent, very Back Bay. Obviously not someone a man like Grosvener would trust with anything important.

"You can transfer me to Mr. Grosvener's office. I have something he wants very much. Something worth a lot of money."

"May I ask what this thing might be?" Expecting to hear about a new perpetual motion machine or another scheme for running cars on water.

"I am the president of the Mela Corporation, please stop wasting my time. If Mr. Grosvener finds you've been delaying his access to several billion dollars he will be quite upset with you."

This got me connected to someone much higher in the organization, Mr. Cary, full of apologies for keeping me waiting. He knew who I was, congratulated me on winning the case. Incredibly, he knew I'd bought those five million shares. This outfit didn't double their share price every year for decades by being out of the know, even if they did live in Wisconsin.

"I can guess why you might like to talk to the boss," he confided, "but perhaps you'd confirm it so we can proceed?"

"You understand the need for absolute complete confidentiality?" I asked, unnecessarily perhaps.

"Of course."

"Mr. Grosvener has been looking for an auto parts operation to fill out that side of his business. There hasn't been one on the market, in fact there aren't many independents left. I might know where there's one which might come up for a reasonable consideration."

"Ah, yes. That's what I thought. Can you come and explain the deal personally?"

"Of course. If I charter a jet out of LAX I can be there this evening. Is there a possibility of Mr. Grosvener and his staff being my guests for dinner? I don't know what Madison has to offer, perhaps you could arrange it?"

And so it was arranged. I waited until Leah had drunk the orange juice and started on the coffee. "You'll have to get dressed soon," I told her gently, "we're going to Wisconsin in a few minutes."

She stared at me with that 'why did I pick this to marry when there were so many others to choose from' look which husbands know so well.

"I suppose you think that's funny," she snarled.

Chapter 21

Mary turned up looking for sisterly sympathy. Instead she got to help pack to my specifications.

"Wear a traveling outfit for today, pack a dress suitable for the hostess of an important business meeting tonight, not too formal for Madison Wisconsin, but wear your jewelry. You can wear the same suit back tomorrow." This ridiculous suggestion deserved the contempt it got. I had to elaborate on the number and credit rating of the attendees, information apparently vital to making the proper selection.

We got to Madison in plenty of time, even with the time difference. Shakespeare-Grosvener kindly sent a company car to meet us, waiting at the general aviation terminal when we arrived. We checked into the Coachman's Golf Resort where, the chauffeur assured us, Mr. Grosvener liked to eat at the restaurant.

Fred Cary had specified 'casual' for dinner. I wore my Paris-made two piece silk suit with the matching white polo-neck shirt. There was however nothing casual about Leah's battle dress. Her diamonds of course, a stunning gown I didn't think I'd seen before but was afraid to ask, just a little makeup to make a wife the President of an up-and-coming high-tech company could be proud of. We strolled to the restaurant ten minutes early as befitted the hosts but the Carys were there before us. Fred introduced his wife Roxana. Her eyes flickered for a moment over Leah's gown, Leah's eyes dwelled for an instant on Roxana's diamond earrings. An invisible electric spark of mutual hostility passed between them. Fortunately the Grosveners appeared before hostilities broke out. He looked in person exactly as he does on TV, with the innocent 'I'm just a Wisconsin farm boy' persona which fools nobody. Mrs. Grosvener looked exactly like what she was, the beloved grandmother of a large tribe of unruly children. She and Leah took to each other instantly.

"My dear," she said, "where did you get that dress?"

"I had it made for me by Rene Belaire in Paris, he does all my things." She turned with an air of innocent helpfulness to Roxana, dressed in the best Madison had to offer. "You should try him," she told her sweetly.

Bloodshed was averted by the manager coming to escort us to our table. No mere headwaiter would do for a party containing someone who could probably buy Madison if he wanted. A large bowl of boiled shrimp in the shell started the evening, with a dry white wine. Mr. Grosvener got the first one peeled before he asked "Now, tell me what you have in mind young man." I guess to him everybody was young.

I got straight to the heart of the matter. "I'd like you to lend me one or two billion dollars," I said.

He went placidly on peeling shrimp. "Now why in the world would I do that?"

I almost said 'because I bought dinner' but decided I didn't know him well enough yet. His next remark sounded like mind reading "And just buying dinner isn't enough reason for my stockholders."

This time I did say it. "Well, I think it's going to be quite a good dinner. But I have another reason. I understand you would like a major auto parts producer to fill out your accessory division enough to make it a major player, on the scale you like your operations to be. I may have one to sell, at a reasonable price."

He got ahead of me again. "Ah, you plan to take over SQV then sell me the automotive group, is that right?"

"That's the essence," I replied, "but the details are a little more complicated."

"I'm sure they are, tell me first what your interest in this is. Apart from a certain antipathy toward SQV management."

This guy knows everything, I thought. The French onion soup appeared to follow the shrimp. I can't remember the wine with it, in any case I kept down to sips. Dealing with loveable old Mr. Grosvener needed all the wits I had. I continued laying out my scheme.

"I need a large going electronic operation with a base of government contracts, people who understand the bidding and contract process. Existing facilities, a specification structure, all the details it would take years and millions to set up from scratch. Then we can make a serious start on commercial development of Dr Jenkin's system."

"With the royalties from Terreau to support your cash flow?" Christ, he does know everything.

"Precisely," I nodded. "I've studied the SQV financials very carefully, analyzed them to see what the groups are worth separately. What I find most interesting is that looked at my way the automotive group contributed about a dollar sixty to the company's last year's reported earnings of a dollar fifty."

"In fact you claim the auto group is worth more than the present market cap of the whole company?"

"Yes," I went on, "particularly now circumstances have dropped their stock price below twenty."

He chuckled. "My impression is that circumstances had a little help in this."

The soup disappeared to be replaced by filet mignon wrapped in bacon. Mrs. Grosvener interrupted the business meeting. "Now men, stop talking for a minute and enjoy this," to her husband, "it's your favorite, don't neglect it."

"My wife is quite right, we should enjoy the dinner. I believe I'm going to accept your proposition if we can work out the details. I need to hear much more about how you're going to do all this. I'd like you, and your charming wife of course, to be my guests for a few days while we have some sessions with my staff."

Leah gave a soft squawk. I patted her hand, answered for us. "We'd be deeply honored of course, but we only brought overnight things, I have a jet waiting to take us back to LA. In any case . . . " I hesitated to tell him the other reason. "Go on," he said.

"We're dangerous people to have around. SQV considers kidnapping, arson, and breaking my corporate attorney's leg, normal business practice. They have no reason to feel any fonder of me after the trial and the filing of the countersuit than before, so I don't want to bring the possibility of violence to your home."

"Harold!" Mrs. Grosvener took over. "Eat your steak and talk later."

I did enjoy the rest of the meal. There's something about rising from the hundred million-dollar class to the billion-dollar class in two courses which raises one's self esteem considerably. Leah, I decided, should have some new earrings. We moved to the lounge for liqueur and coffee. I felt only appreciation when a sip of the glass that appeared in front of me proved it to be Chivas Regal. Shakespeare-Grosvener must have an intelligence system rivaling the CIA.

The ladies formed their own group when Mrs. Grosvener, Mildred to her friends, asked Leah what she had been doing in Paris. Harold resumed the discussion.

"Come back to my place, I think I have reasonable security there, you don't need to worry about assassins. Mildred can take Leah shopping tomorrow in Madison for what she needs. Send your jet back, I'll get you back to LA when we're through. I like to take my time looking at the details, don't rush me."

"Well, that's very kind of you, of course we'd be delighted."

"Fred, do you have any questions we ought to think about now?" Harold asked.

"Yes, I'd just like to hear a little more about how you plan to take SQV over, and why you don't think other parties wouldn't get into a bidding war once you put SQV in play."

"As to the bidding war," I answered, "another party would be faced with an unknown liability in my suit against SQV. Remember they obviously and publicly perjured themselves. If I take them over the suit is moot." Fred nodded. I went on, "and in a sense I plan to print the money to buy SQV. Mela will have its IPO in a few days. We only plan to raise about three units, but we'll have established a market value for our stock." A 'unit' in Texas talk is one hundred million dollars.

Harold nodded. "And should you lose a bidding war the profit on your five million shares would sooth your feelings, wouldn't they? That's enough for tonight, we can go into it tomorrow at my office."

He certainly did have an adequate security at his estate. Massive electrically operated gates with an armed guard in the gatehouse, a brick wall topped with barbed wire stretching away apparently for miles. I almost asked him what his defenses against helicopter attack might be, but it didn't seem like the right thing somehow. I found the interior a bit overwhelming, the ceilings too high and the rooms too big, but it is an impressive house. Mansion.

Go into it we did next day at his office, hours of questions, many from bright young B school grads trying to prove any scheme they hadn't thought of couldn't be any good. My MBA from USC got me some respect from this section, taken long ago by the standards of these children who didn't look old enough to have driving licenses. A few of the professors I had studied under were still at USC, so I had something in common with a couple of the inquisitors.

The essence of my plan didn't need much explaining. I'd buy control of SQV with borrowed Shakespeare-Grosvener money, pledging the auto parts group against the loan. Then when I had control of the board I'd sell the company to Mela for stock, sell Harold the parts he wanted, and settle down to make the remainder profitable again so we could exploit the Finder technology properly without worrying about where the next penny, or hundred million dollars, was coming from.

There were questions on why I thought the IPO would be successful enough to support all this. I told them it would be a surprise, I'd send them invitations to the press conference that would do it. I also suggested they might read the current 'Archeology Today' but that wasn't in their mental set.

By the end of the day I felt as if I'd spent it in the lions den. A little girl in a business suit asked me, in tones suggesting she thought I couldn't read a balance sheet, "How did you conclude SQV other than the auto group was losing money? I couldn't see it." Implying if she couldn't it wasn't there.

I gritted my teeth and fought down various unusable answers. "Actually, it's not too hard to find if you look at it from the point of view of two separate groups which should each be making a profit. There are two places it's buried. First, they have a monstrous G&A," that's general and administrative overhead in case you didn't know, "partly because they've got some expenses in it which should be shown as expense to the groups, and because they have a bloated and unnecessary headquarters staff in New York. Where they don't even have an operation. They've managed to assign a disproportionate share of the G&A to the auto group, I suspect with the connivance of the government to keep the price of the military contracts down."

"And you think the split company wouldn't have the sort of G&A they do?"

"I'm damn sure my part wouldn't, and somehow I can't see Harold permitting it in his part. As soon as I sell off the auto group I'll close the New York office altogether, which'll save a significant amount of money right away. The rest is a bit subtler. They have several losing divisions on a cash flow basis but they're treating the losses as capital expense, value of research, that sort of thing. Some of the divisions don't even really fit their overall business as far as I can see, so I'm not sure why they're doing it. My business plans are a lot more direct and straightforward so I'd scrap these divisions and transfer any profitable lines to others. Not that I'd have so many separate ones anyway."

"Very well," announced Harold, "that's enough for one day. Tomorrow you can meet with some of my people to sign some papers. Is there anything else you want?"

"Yes, I think there is. Your staff has a great deal more experience with takeovers than I do, is there any chance of borrowing someone as a consultant? That would give you a window into what's going on too, without having meetings on it."

Which is how the Carys came to live temporarily in LA. I hoped Roxana would enjoy it. I didn't need to worry. Back at the Grosveners for dinner Leah confided that Roxana was really quite nice when you got to know her. They'd spent the day with Mildred and got to know each other. Good for Mildred I thought, Harold wasn't the only smart one in the family.

Safely returned to LA I thought I deserved a rest, but the next order of business was to inflate the price of Mela stock so our IPO would put us in a position to buy SQV with paper we printed.

Chapter 22

"Why," Leah asked on the way back, "are we living in a hotel?"

"Where would you like to live?"

"You have that beach house, what's wrong with that?"

"Ah. Yes. Two things," I hesitated, "the obvious one is there's no maid service, nobody to make the beds each day, no room service."

"I can make beds," Leah said, " even call for meals to get delivered. Cook, if I absolutely have to"

"Alright, the other reason is it belongs to an old life I don't have any more, I don't want any more. I wasn't married when I lived there. I was another person. "

"Didn't you used to have a Mercedes?"

"Christ, I'd forgotten that. I suppose it's been sitting in the garage, if it got returned."

"Let's go look at the house. What are you afraid of?"

I thought about it. "I think I'm afraid of meeting my old self there," I finally managed to say.

"Well, let's go exorcise your ghost. It's a pity we don't have the Celestine too, for trips to Catalina."

"Hell, I've got a yacht, the *Splendor Hyaline*, in Marina yacht club. I'd even forgotten that."

"The *what*?"

"Oh, it's the name of the ship in one of the C S Lewis stories I read over and over as a boy. Has a nice ring to it, doesn't it?"

"We'll go look at that too when we have time."

I'd forgotten she'd never seen my yacht, she joined our happy band on the Mela Mermaid as was.

Safely back, changed, unpacked, and refreshed we set off to my Malibu beach house, once the most desirable residence I could think of. One Pinkerton man drove, the other rode shotgun. They took their job very seriously. So did I.

The minute parking space outside the garage just had room for us. I walked up to the front door, reached in the crevice in the planter where the spare key lived, and went to open the door. "Excuse me sir," said one of our bodyguards, "let me do that."

I stood aside while he opened the door and looked round the house. Empty. The cleaning service must still be coming once a week to dust and vacuum, the place looked clean enough. It also, to my new eye, looked tawdry, tacky, looked like a slightly run-down bachelor pad. Which of course it was. The mis-matched rattan furniture, the dubious prints on the walls, all belonged to some stranger. Leah wandered all through, admired the view off the deck, which indeed was the best part of the house. Her inspection finished, she pronounced judgement.

"I love it, perfect for us. I could make a home out of this. The man who redecorated the boat, we could get him over to do it. Make some alterations, have a much better kitchen and bathrooms. Close in that deck, make a new room out of it."

"You really like it? You'd like to live here? I didn't know that was a man, I decided it was a woman. He or she did a good job on the boat though. Does he or she speak English?"

Leah thought about it. "I don't think so, never heard him. Now you mention it, I'm not sure. Maybe it is a woman. Doesn't matter, we need an interior decorator and that's a good one. I'll call him to come over."

Now not too long ago my mind would have boggled at the idea of calling an interior decorator to come over from Paris to redo my Malibu beach house. Just shows how quickly one can adjust to being a billionaire. Even if the money is borrowed.

"Show me your car," Leah commanded.

I opened the door to the garage. There stood a very dusty Mercedes with one flat rear tire. Peering into the windows I saw the keys on the drivers seat. The doors were locked. "Hell," I said, "I've no idea where the spare keys are. Why did she go and lock it? I'll have to break the window."

"Go on, get them to come and take this one away and bring a newer one." Leah had got used to big money in a hurry. Associating with the Grosveners had expanded her horizons.

"OK, see if there's things to make coffee with, get the Pinkertons to sit and relax and have some while I see what the

Mercedes dealer can do. I don't think I want another yet, I'll get this one taken away then we can look at new ones later."

It took twenty minutes for the tow truck to arrive, from a dealer hot to sell me a new car. We backed the car we came in out so it partly blocked Pacific Coast Highway, to the indignation of a whole lot of traffic. The tow truck, or I expect as it came from the Mercedes dealer, the distressed vehicle recovery system, backed up to my old one and pulled it backward out of the garage with its tail in the air. It bumped over the curb as the driver cut too sharp to avoid the remaining lanes of traffic.

The front of the car lit up with a brilliant white light so powerful I could feel the heat on my face like the sun. After a few seconds it died out to be replaced by swirling orange flame. The windows burst to let tongues of flame come boiling out over the roof. Our two bodyguards hustled us back out of range, and the tow truck driver came running up to join us. "What the fuck was that?" I asked.

"Thermite bomb," one of the Pinkertons answered tersely.

We had now managed to bring PCH to a complete standstill in both directions, making it impossible for the fire department to get to us. I put my arms round Leah. "I'm not sure redecorating is all we're going to need," I told her. Police eventually managed to get through and directed the traffic into two lanes on the other side of the road. The fire truck came and sprayed foam on everything, to the detriment of the tow truck, the front of my house, and assorted innocent bystanders. A news helicopter came. Once the foam dribbled off so I could see the remains I decided it probably wasn't worth much as a trade-in any more. What an exciting day we were having. The police of course blamed me for the whole thing. They remembered me from the old days.

Over dinner that night with the rest of the active board of the Mela Corporation I gave a spirited account of our day, including an impersonation of a police sergeant trying to get me to admit I'd set a bomb off in my own car. Leah got more and more thoughtful. She came up with rather a sobering question.

"Did anybody at all know you'd lost your spare keys?"

"Well, they're not exactly lost. They must be in the house somewhere."

"That's what I mean. Whoever set that bomb expected you to get the spare keys, get in the car, and drive it out. The flat tire and the lost keys spoiled that, but what would have happened otherwise?"

"Hmm," I answered more soberly, "you would be a rich charming widow right now. Or if you'd been with me we would be together in the Elysian fields."

Mary fired up. "This is ridiculous. Why don't we start throwing bombs and beating people up? Let's burn SQV down."

"Let's not," I objected, "we may need it. I don't know, we're planning a bad end for their management but it doesn't include violence. Yet. After we get through with all we're trying, then we can get vengeful. Right now all we can do is be careful, use Pinkerton, don't trust anyone who's not at this table."

In the next few days airfreight delivered a whole lot of crates from Paris, passing through customs as TV studio monitor equipment. I rented the hotels largest assembly room, and had an armed full time guard put on it. Joe with the hindrance of a crew of Union electricians put together a nice new Terreau version of the Finder display system, much bigger than the prototype on the Belle Celestine. The press and TV were invited to a thrilling demonstration, timed for shortly before our IPO. Just for fun I invited the Navy too. The Carys arrived from Madison in time to see it.

The hotel provided drinks and snacks, always guaranteed to get the press well represented. Our show started at one o'clock, so the TV could hit the evening news. I started it off, told them we had a new underwater survey system which would revolutionize whole business and scientific fields. They yawned, got more drinks. I explained that Terreau had made the prototype we were going to demonstrate in France under license, because of SQV's interference, culminating in their humiliation in their unsuccessful suit. If we'd provided chairs they'd have snored. Then I introduced Dr Jenkins, which got a flicker of interest. He turned the equipment on, though really it had been on all along, just in sleep mode. The box came alive with a slow sweep over a wrecked battleship. The crowd surged forward to get a better view. Hologram after hologram floated through the box, fish, whales, ancient wrecks, modern wrecks, and the railroad loco upside down. I think everyone there tried to touch the image. Some of them even put their drinks down. The TV crew tried desperately to find some way to show the 3-D effect, but couldn't from a distance. I told them to wait until the party was over, we'd try getting them in close to see if the effect could be enhanced. A huge success, just what we needed to create some demand for our IPO. Which, of course, wasn't mentioned. We handed out information packages as the reporters left, including a copy of Archeology Today. The equipment went back to airfreight under armed guard to return to Terreau immediately the show finished.

The pictures came out quite well on TV, getting the camera in close and moving it around really showing the images off. The commentator didn't know what to make of it, but used the words I loved to hear-'invention of the century.' Maybe we'd priced the IPO too low. Not that it mattered, the important thing would be the price the stock settled at in public trading. That, you see, would be instead of money to buy SQV so the higher it went the better. The market cap of SQV still amounted to almost three billion dollars, so we needed a lot of scrip to buy it outright. Mela stock at forty would be about the least that would work.

Next morning I called the Rodeo Drive branch of the jewelry store Leah patronized in Paris. You know, 'Ah Madame, a pleasure to see Madame, please to come through to the private viewing room, let me take Madame's coat and purse, Marcel, a chair for Madame, a little white wine for Madame? And what may we have the pleasure of showing Madame today?' I wondered what the American branch would be like. I told them of course that Madame was a customer of their Paris store, with every faith they would be exchanging emails on the subject the moment I put the phone down. Then I told him what I wanted.

"I'd like to see some diamond earrings, nice white stones, no flaws, investment grade in fact. Something notable but in good taste. If you don't have any made, show us some suitable stones and we'll see about having you mount them. Would this afternoon be too soon?"

I gathered that right now would be fine, anytime of the night or day in fact. Two this afternoon I told him would do nicely. I don't need to describe our reception. We felt right at home, down to Leah's favorite white wine on the little table thoughtfully provided for writing checks. After a decent pause for conversation, all in French, a velvet tray appeared with a pair of earrings on it. Leah looked blankly at them, mentally comparing the weight and quality of the stones with those in a certain pair she'd seen in Madison. "Er," she said.

"Madame would like to see some more notable," I translated.

Another pair appeared on a different tray. Leah looked at them with pursed lips.

"Non?"

"Non."

So the afternoon wore on, sipping wine, practicing my French, watching Leah's face as the parade passed in front of her. This of course is part of the process, the slow work up to the really expensive part. I could tell when the climax approached. A certain quickening of the staff fetching and carrying, a new bottle of wine in case the old had become warm, a fresh glass for Madame. Would M'sieur prefer a Chivas? When the manager, surely not just any old salesman, thought the moment had come, a French girl almost the equal of Celestine tripped in with a beautiful case. She opened it with a flourish and presented it for Madame's inspection.

"Ooooh," said Madame.

After that it only remained to step discreetly aside with the manager to settle the sordid details while a whole bevy of French ladies gathered round Madame to fit her new earrings. "Perhaps M'sieur would like us to add this to his account with our Paris branch?"

Perhaps M'sieur would like to know how much M'sieur had just spent. M'sieur, billion dollars or not, was quite surprised. "Madame must be very special," the manager said with a leer. Seemed to me Madame was going to need an armed guard every time Madame wore her new earrings.

Madame's gratitude, I am happy to report, was indeed very special.

Chapter 23

The Mela Corporation, as befitted its new standing in the world, rented the top floor of a new building in Torrance for temporary offices. They were ready in time for the IPO. We really needed a Director of Finance, particularly to fend off the IRS, but I had a good reason for delaying that. Instead I hired a well-known accounting company to fill in temporarily.

I have never, of course, had a baby, so do not know exactly how it feels, but I believe the days before the IPO gave me some insight into it. I paced about, did unnecessary jobs, bothered my crew with disjointed conversations, fussed over the logo design for Mela, thought of all the people I might call but didn't call them. Fred Cary said I was acting about normal, or a little more so. Leah, encouraged by those around me with work to do, decided we should go on a sightseeing trip until it was all over. A good long way away, my friends suggested. She took me on a Sonoma wine country tour, by coach, to the outspoken alarm of Pinkerton. Leah put my gun in her purse to satisfy them. Part way through she took my telephone away from me. I really enjoyed it after that, got into the spirit of the thing, made amateur comments on the samples laid out for us, appreciated the size of the barrels each winery so proudly showed as the biggest in the state. The awful truth is that California wines are at least the equals of French, better in many cases. And more consistent.

Leah let me come back to LA after the market closed on issue day. I hardly dared look at the results, while my grinning and already half potted board stood watching me. Mela stock, NASD symbol MELA, closed at 249.50. Took me a few seconds to understand where the decimal was.

Joe and I each owned 26% of the corporation, twenty-six million shares. At $249.50 each that gave us a paper worth of – Ooooh.

Harold called from Madison to congratulate us.

"I hope you got your allotment of the stock OK?" I asked him. He chuckled. "Of course."

"I have the impression someone has been buying SQV stock, moderate quantities a bit at a time. That wouldn't count as insider trading, would it?"

He chuckled again. "My dear boy, I'm not an insider, and what makes you think I'm buying SQV?" I guess his 400% profit in one day on the Mela stock had promoted me to a 'dear boy.'

"Oh, I don't know. Someone with foresight and capital might see their depressed price as a bottom fishing opportunity, that's all. I hope whoever that purchaser is I can count on his proxies if we get hostile?"

"Oh, I'm sure you can. Cary is there to look after my interests."

I may not have Shakespeare-Grosvener's intelligence system, but I do have some contact with what's going on.

We provided a gala dinner that night, in a private room of the hotel. Everybody involved came, Mela corporation in strength down to our new secretarial staff, the Carys, as many elected officials as we could get, my broker, Jerry my yacht broker and his current significant other, some bankers who had got paid a great deal of money for midwifery, several people who I didn't recognize. Assorted wives and others.

Leah wore her new earrings, which fascinated the bankers present, Mary wore a gown that I thought went a bit far, which fascinated every other male. Not that Leah wasn't showing a fair bit of cleavage to draw attention to her necklace. Or perhaps the other way round. I felt very proud of her, carrying her position as hostess and Wife of the President very graciously. Joe hadn't quite come out of shock. Here he had become one of the richest men in the country apparently overnight, had the most charming person present next to Leah clinging to him, and found himself being treated with respect and deference by some important people. And not, this time, for his engineering skills. Roxana Cary's earrings now came second, which might augur ill for Fred's financial future. I had a consolation for Roxana. As I circulated with pre-dinner cocktails I made a suggestion to the Carys.

"SQV is going to get even more hostile when our 'friendly' initial takeover offer arrives, let alone when we start the hostile tender action. How about letting Leah and Roxana take a trip to Paris to do some shopping, out of reach?"

"You want to get rid of me?" Leah objected.

"No dear, that 's just it. I don't want to get rid of you. I remember that Thermite bomb and checking to see if you were breathing when I found you after your Canadian trip. I think in fact that you, Roxana, Mary, and Celestine would be a lot safer far way with Terreau security watching out for you. We'll miss you terribly, but not as much as we will if SQV gets hold of you. In fact it might be better if Joe went too, he's got plenty to do over there."

They all saw the merit of the idea, particularly Roxana with visions of Paris couturiers. I whispered to Leah "There's nothing to stop me jetting over for a naughty French weekend once in a while." She gave a delicious wriggle against me and said "Mmmm."

The dinner went splendidly. Everyone had a good time, and why not as many of them had become modestly financially secure today. The later details are a bit hazy in my mind, but I do remember having my hand shaken by several politicians with visions of contributions to their next election expenses.

Once the Paris party was safely out of the way we sent our friendly takeover offer to SQV's board. We very reasonably offered to exchange all SQV stock for Mela Corporation, thirteen SQV for one Mela. We didn't expect them to accept it of course, even if it had been a fair offer they would have turned it down. They had to go through the motions of considering it, before rejecting the offer as "Not in the best interests of the stockholders." Our next move, prepared in advance and cleared with the SEC, was to make a hostile tender offer for enough SQV stock to gain control of the board. Fred had a pleasant surprise on this.

"I've managed to persuade some of the institutional investors to give me proxies. Once they heard the deal we were planning and knew Harold had a hand in it they figured they would make more money with us in charge than the present management."

"Go on," I encouraged him, "how many shares have you got proxies for?"

His answer brightened my day considerably. "Oh, about twenty-five million."

Now that was over a quarter of their total outstanding, so we probably had control right now, with Mela's five million. Still, better to make absolutely sure. Especially as the money came from Shakespeare-Grosvener.

The market couldn't figure out where the affair might go, so Mela stock dropped to 225, while SQV rose to 22. Only to be expected, we'd have to pay more than that to get control. As we needed less than twenty million more shares to have voting control no matter what any other stockholder might want the price could go a lot higher without it becoming a problem. I thought SQV seemed to be taking our attack very calmly, I'd expected more of a reaction from them.

I felt very pleased with myself when I left our Torrance office to go back to the hotel. Everything under control, our plans working out nicely. As I stood waiting on the sidewalk for the car to come round for me I noticed an old Chevy cruising slowly down Torrance Boulevard. As it came opposite me a young Chicano leaned out of the window toward me. Too late I saw the gun in his hand.

I remember very distinctly the dreamy slow motion sensation of something hitting me a tremendous blow in the chest. What a pity, I thought, I was really enjoying life. A brief vision of Leah in black flitted before me then just nothing.

No time passed for me. I'd closed my eyes falling to the pavement outside my office, opened them again lying uncomfortably on a hard bed. Very thirsty, feeling very sick. I felt mentally around my body to see what I still had, realized I didn't need to breathe, something did it for me. Very relaxing. My hands hurt, because of the tubes I could see plugged into the backs of them, leading off to somewhere I'd have to move my head to see. My chest hurt all over, burning. Too much effort to move. Just lie and let something breathe. I couldn't remember then what had put me there, too hard to think about. I must have moved, because someone leaned over to look into my face. It seemed to be Leah, in black. Ah, I thought, that explains it. I'm dead, that's why I don't have to breathe. Then the darkness came back.

I decided, next time I woke up, that I couldn't be dead, if I were dead I wouldn't hurt so much. Leah leaned over me again, It really was her, not in black but something dark, her face drawn and white, her hair tangled and fuzzy. She looked adorable. I tried to speak, couldn't.

"Keep still, I'll call the doctor," she whispered.

I woke up again to find a fatherly person in a white coat bending over me instead of Leah. He looked a lot more cheerful than Leah had.

"Ah, good, good, we're awake are we?" Silly question.

I croaked something, very hard to talk when you can't draw breath to time.

"I think we might see if you can breathe on your own. I'm going to turn the machine off for a moment. I'll put it back on if there's any distress." Weird sense of humor, this man who ever he might be. I liked not breathing, too much effort to do it for myself.

After a moment I very reluctantly tried breathing in. The pain in my chest felt like a knife in my side. I could speak now though. "Oh, shit," I said.

"I expect the incisions drag a little, that'll pass. I'll give you something to help."

Drag a little? Very funny. A nurse appeared to inject something, not into me but into the IV bottle on my right. A warm glow spread through me. Breathing isn't so bad, I thought.

"Thirsty," I mumbled. Leah pushed a straw into my mouth. I sucked on it. Good, stale warm water, my favorite.

I lay for a moment composing my next remark, too much effort to waste words. "The takeover, the tender offer . . . "

Leah answered. "It should go out any day, Fred took over for you, he's offering to buy up to twenty million for cash at 30."

I went back to sleep.

Chapter 24

I'll spare you the sordid details, the diapers, the painful sessions spitting up blood clots, changing IVs, being washed in bed. I got to see my scars, very impressive. As each day and long night went by I stayed awake a little longer, took first liquid then some baby food. Leah stayed with me until she looked almost as bad as I did. I asked for my phone, wanted to check the market, wanted to know how the tender offer went. Leah didn't know, certainly wouldn't let me have the telephone, said surfing the Web on a little screen worrying about stock prices wouldn't help me get better.

When I got coherent enough to ask sensible questions I had some for the doctor.

"How come," I asked him, "I'm alive when I distinctly remember getting shot in the chest?"

"You were very lucky," he told me, "your bodyguards acted most promptly. Instead of waiting for an ambulance they threw you in the car and drove the two blocks to the hospital."

"Ah, this must be Torrance Memorial?"

"Yes, of course. You bled out of the exit wounds, instead of drowning in your own blood. You almost bled to death before we got you, I should think the car will need reupholstering." He smiled to show he thought this was funny. Didn't strike me that way. "You stopped breathing but we put a tube in the good lung while we repaired the damage. Kept adding blood transfusions, used quite a lot on you." Smiling again dammit, macabre sense of human these people have. "Your heart stopped a couple of times but we were in there anyway so we worked it manually until it picked up on its own."

"So I died several times?"

"In a sense, but we don't give up on anybody who still has brain activity."

"Now, after all that jolly description, am I going to get better?"

"Hmm. We were concerned about brain damage of course, but I see no signs of it. Then the danger was infection, but that usually shows up in the first few days, and the incisions are healing nicely."

"Go on," I insisted, "but?"

"This much damage is always unpredictable. You'll have lost some lung function, can't say how much but you've still got one good lung. We had to remake two ribs, so I don't think you'll be doing any heavy lifting for a while. I'm a bit puzzled by the injuries, because after the first broken rib there seem to be at least two damage trails. We don't have the bullet, both trails left exit wounds, one broke another rib. One touched your heart, one went through your left lung. Very interesting. I wonder if the bullet was a ceramic device, supposed to break up and spray pieces all through you. It didn't, perhaps the muzzle velocity was too low, too short a barrel or a home made load filled short. The heart repair will heal up I think, but it'll take time to get that back to normal. On the whole I think the prognostication is favorable. Oh yes, I think so."

That, I thought, was altogether more than I wanted to know about it. Didn't sound to me like a ringing endorsement of my rapid return to health. A question came to me.

"If the bullet had worked, what would have happened?"

"Ah, well, hard to say exactly, it's not something we see often. If it had shrapnelled you would have had little pieces penetrating a good deal of your internal organs. Not necessarily immediately fatal, but inevitably so in time."

"So someone really hates me, don't they?"

He said he couldn't speculate on that, not a medical matter.

"I've got a lot of unfinished business, when can I have a board meeting in here?"

"Oh, now, you can't sit up yet, you won't be ready to get back to work for quite a while."

That's all he knew. William and Mike came as soon as I could persuade Leah to send for them. At that I had to fall back on the claim I'd be worse off worrying about it than getting all the news first hand.

"Give," I commanded weakly, "tell me everything that's happened."

They did, all good news. The tender had been oversubscribed, a lot of people wanted out of SQV and our price looked like the best they were likely to get. We'd offered the same as the stock was before the disastrous trial. Twenty million shares at thirty was . . . took me a while to work it out. Six hundred million, much less than we'd borrowed. Thanks to Fred's proxies. Mela stock had taken a hit when the offer came out, which they assured me was normal. The low was 150, still well in the range. It had drifted back up to 200. Very good.

"Now we need to elect a new board, vote the next phase. How do we do that?" The doctor was right, this made me very tired, but I had to keep on. The cold rage against SQV management, whoever had decided that killing me would discourage the takeover, kept me running. They weren't going to win. I tried to get another question out but the words got tangled.

"Can I when do it? I wanna have the meeting in New . . . " I forgot what I was trying to say.

"Don't worry, Fred has it all set up. We'll meet in New York, you sign a proxy for us and we . . ." But I'd gone to sleep.

I got to sit up, which produced some more interesting coughing, then graduated to real food. The IV came out, leaving the back of my hand black and yellow. Leah got some sleep, came in looking more like her proper self. I got some tickle and squeak that I much needed. I saw the armed guard sitting in a chair outside my door, night and day. I decided privately there was no way I would miss the pleasure of chairing the first and last meeting of the new SQV board of directors, so when I was alone started to try standing up a little, very scary at first. Then a step away from the bed. Then I made it to the bathroom by myself. Of course, that was only three steps, but a long way for me.

The doctor noticed I looked relatively chipper, announced proudly that I might try getting out of bed. I thanked him profusely. After he'd gone I sent Leah to the hospital drug store for a walking stick. I slid out of bed and put my arms round her, kissed her everywhere I could reach. "Wow," she said, "you are getting better, aren't you?"

"Get me a robe, I'm going for a walk."

She got me a robe, thought I was joking about a walk. The stick helped a lot, not so much for walking as to rest by leaning on it. That time I made about twenty feet before I came over all trembly and had to be helped back by an indignant nurse.

Once safely in bed I asked for my phone back, I had work to do. "Tomorrow," Leah promised.

Tomorrow I called Fred to announce they weren't getting any proxy from me, they were getting me in person. Took the crew less than five minutes to get to the hospital to see if I'd gone crazy. William, Mike, and Fred brushed nurses aside to make an out-of-hours visit. "What's this nonsense about going to New York for the meeting?" they wanted to know. I got out of bed, put on my own dressing gown, and lead them to the patient's lounge to show I could walk on my own. This room, furnished with lumpy armchairs, offered all the delights usually provided for convalescents, jigsaw puzzles missing key pieces, forty-nine card decks, a television set which only seemed to get soap operas, ancient magazines with the good parts torn out. The perfect place for a board meeting of a multi-billion dollar corporation.

I waved my stick at them. "You can see I'm perfectly fit, ready to chair the meeting I've been dreaming about. Nobody's going to deprive me of the pleasure of expelling the SQV management."

The chorus of concern that I obviously wasn't nearly well enough to fly to New York and work yet brought the head nurse to keep order. "Go away," I told her, "or we'll buy this hospital and do what we like."

"You just do that," she replied with steely eye and commanding mien, "but right now you'll make less noise or I'll throw you all out personally."

"Nurse, you tell them, tell them I'm perfectly well enough to fly to New York for a holiday."

She glared at me. "We'll just see what the doctor has to say about all this."

The doctor had a lot to say, all amounting to "out of the question."

"How about if you come with me, and a nurse. You can look after me every minute. Almost every minute," I added, thinking about Leah.

"You're really serious, aren't you?"

"You bet. Is it a deal?"

"Certainly not, I've got other patients beside you. If you're really bent on doing it I could find an intern and a nurse to go with you, but it's at your own risk you understand."

So a week later saw us all on a chartered jet to New York and the SQV board room. I got wheeled about through airports and hotels, very very tired by the time I got put to bed. Leah slept with me but I'm ashamed to say I was too tired to do anything about it. That night.

SQV's New York offices astounded me. There were pictures on the walls I recognized from illustrations in books, deep carpets, and expensive furniture. The female staff looked as if they'd been rented from an expensive call girl operation. I made a triumphal entry in a wheelchair flanked by two Pinkerton men. We swept in and demanded to be shown to the boardroom. There the old board sat waiting for us. "Now gentlemen . . ." the chairman started. This was my day.

"We are the owners of this corporation, representing a majority of the stockholders. A new board has been duly elected and I am the chairman. You gentlemen may go."

They started to protest. People in shock often have trouble accepting reality. I didn't know if any of these people were personally responsible for the damage done to me and others, but they must surely have connived in it. "I'll ask these good men," indicating my guards, both big strong fellows, "to help you out if you have trouble on your own."

They left, shouting and complaining through the plush offices. One of the Pinkerton men escorted them to the door. We sat. Of course I was already sitting, but this was official. "Leah, if you'd be kind enough to keep minutes? Now the first order of business is to consider the offer from the Mela Corporation to buy SQV for one share of Mela stock to five shares of SQV. This offer seems to me generous in the extreme, as it values SQV at forty dollars a share, a twenty-dollar premium over the present market. Any discussion? No? All in favor? Any against? Then William, please start the formalities of issuing Mela stock to the SQV shareholders. Next business, nominations for the President and CEO of the new Mela corporation. Thank you, all in favor? Against? I appreciate the honor." I did enjoy this. "Next the question of disposing of the automotive group of the Mela Corporation. This business line doesn't fit our plans for the future, I propose we sell it at once. We have an offer on the table, represented by Fred." Perhaps I should have mentioned that we had decided Fred would be a great asset to the board.

Fred solemnly read out Shakespeare-Grosvener's offer. "Harold offers to buy the automotive group complete as a going concern for three billion dollars, paid as follows. Cash advanced, fees etc already incurred, six hundred and fifty million dollars, one and a half billion dollars in new cash, and the balance in S-G stock at today's market. Subject to due diligence and Mela Corporation's assumption of any debts of SQV." Fred of course knew we'd agreed this with SQV's bankers before we started the takeover.

"Thank you Fred, Leah are we going too fast for you?"

She shook her head, "I can write really fast when it's something as much fun as this."

"Very well gentlemen, is there any discussion? The price is agreeable?" It had better be, or we'd have made an enemy of Harold which I wouldn't want to do even if I didn't admire him so much personally. "Very well, all in favor? Opposed? Then William you'll start the process in escrow? Any further business? Oh yes, I almost forgot. In light of the illegal and reprehensible acts of personal violence committed by the former management of SQV all officers of the former Corporation other than the auto parts group are dismissed for cause without bonus, severance pay, or other unwarranted charges on the Corporation. Raise your hand to indicate a 'for' vote. Thank you, that is unanimous. Now any further business? And if anybody says yes they will be responsible for me passing out right now, I need a coffee and a rest."

Nobody did. We all shook hand, Leah kissed everybody, coffee was fetched. By some intuition Mike discovered a bar off the boardroom, concealed behind a section of paneling. Not that I encourage drinking on company time you understand, but if ever there was an occasion for it this was it. No Chivas, but some good stuff. Coffee and a brandy refreshed me enough to perform another duty I had been anticipating for weeks.

Chapter 25

A few minutes of relaxing with coffee and a little brandy had me back in fighting trim again. My two bodyguards wheeled me out to the entrance to the president's office. This, believe it or not, had double doors like a damn palace. I got rather shakily out of the chair ready for a formal entrance. The lacquered female at the desk outside objected. "You can't go in there, I have to announce you. He's not seeing anybody today."

I took no notice. My bodyguards flung the doors back for me to stalk in as steadily as possible. The furniture and fitting must have cost millions, one of the pictures hanging behind the desk looked to me like a Monet. I had never met the former president of SQV, he had not thought it necessary to attend the trial in LA. He stood up red faced as we stormed in.

"How dare you, get out of my office at once, I'll have you know I am the president of this corporation and you . . . "

I out-shouted him, leaning on my stick for stability to address the Pinkerton men. "This man no longer works here, please escort him to the door and make sure he does not return. He may take his immediate personal belongings, nothing else."

"You can't do that . . . "

"I am doing it, as the president of the former SQV Corporation by order of the board of directors. Leave quietly now or I'll have you thrown out."

The ignominy of walking past a goggle-eyed crowd of his former subordinates with each arm in the grip of a large uniformed escort began the process of soothing that savage thing peering out of the depths of my brain.

I sat in the red leather chair of the president. It didn't fit me, too big and too soft. One of the buttons on the desk looked promising, so I pressed it. The lacquered female entered with a white face and tears on her cheeks.

"There are six vice presidents who have their offices here. I want to see all of them right now please. If any of them doesn't want to come inform him I'll send an armed escort to enforce my wishes. And ask the rest of my party to be kind enough to join me. Thank you."

"Oh, oh, oh," she said and went back to her desk to start her grim job.

Leah came and felt my head, which I appreciated, "Now don't overdo it, don't make yourself ill, I couldn't stand it again."

The other four were circling the walls admiring the paintings. William knew his art. "That's a Monet, and I swear this is a Cezanne. There's a fortune here."

"Right, a nice addition to our working capital just as soon as I can get Sotheby's to auction them."

An indignant crowd of VPs straggled in. I addressed them. "Listen carefully. Leah, please read the relevant section of the minutes of the recent board meeting to these people."

They stood for a moment in stunned silence, then started to protest. I overrode them "Either leave quietly or I'll have you thrown out, go now."

They went.

I called the remaining staff to the boardroom for their share. The president's office, spacious as it was, didn't have room for the number of the headquarters staff. No wonder their balance sheet had oddities. I got pushed back in my wheelchair. Leah had reason to be concerned, I felt faint and giddy but made one more effort.

"This office is now closed. As of a few minutes ago the telephone number terminated, and calls will route automatically to the Mela offices in LA. Each of you will get whatever severance package you are entitled to by your present employment agreement. You may stay here and wait for them or come back in a few days. All of you will also receive one month's additional pay in lieu of notice. I appreciate this has come as a shock, but the Mela Corporation is closing or selling most of the prior SQV properties and there is no justification for the continuing expense of a New York headquarters office. Does anyone know of a special problem this course presents?"

Silence, broken by sobs. A voice asked "what about the mail?"

"Snailmail is also redirected by the post office to LA, as is email. Anything else?"

Some brave soul wanted to know more. "Why are you doing this to us? Can't we have the choice of moving to LA? Don't you need some of us?"

"I am in this wheelchair because of the efforts of the SQV management to assassinate me, their second unsuccessful attempt. I think it best not to mix unknown SQV employees with Mela Corporation. Also, Mela's business plans are widely divergent from . . . you'll have to excuse me, I'm not ready to continue at the moment." The black closed in on me again. When I came to again I was lying on a couch in the presidential office with Leah fussing over me. "There, wasn't that fun?" I whispered to her. My attendant intern came in, felt my pulse, took my temperature. "Complete rest," he advised, "no stress, no exercise. Definitely no plane rides for a while."

So Leah and I had a brief New York vacation while a company who specialized in such things closed out the SQV offices, sold off the contents, and put the lease up for sale.

Three days later I felt ready to face a plane ride back to LA, with an oxygen tank if I needed it and everybody worrying over me. I wanted to get back to work as soon as I could because I worried about the rate the Defense and Electronics group might be losing money. To run out of working capital while waiting for the sale to Harold to complete would be embarrassing to say the least. William assured me he was watching the bank balances, but I knew how little we really had for the moment. Something in the hundreds of millions wouldn't have counted as 'little' a few months ago, but at our present scale it didn't seem a lot. The bank loans we had assumed were already burdensome, certainly we shouldn't add to them. William made a side trip to Detroit instead of coming back to LA with us. He came back with reassuring news from his interview with the automotive group.

"We're in no danger of running out of money right now," he told us, "we have the cash flow from automotive until the sale closes, the sale proceeds afterwards. If we can get the rest profitable, or at least positive cash flow, in this fiscal year we're in good shape."

I was not in good shape. Joe said that if I didn't go to the doctor for a thorough work over he'd personally carry me there. I spent an uncomfortable day having everything checked that could be, with a spell on the treadmill to see how many miles I could walk up hill. The answer was 'not many.' Hardly any in fact. The doctor insisted Leah hear the verdict after I got dressed.

"How much do you need this man?" he asked her.

"I need him a lot," she answered, "and there are stockholders, banks, and ten thousand workers who need him too. What are we going to do with him?"

"We are going to get him away from work for a complete rest for a long time. I don't like the amount of strain his heart shows, he's anemic, and he's not as tough as he makes out. There are definite symptoms of posttraumatic stress syndrome. Bad dreams, disturbed nights I expect?"

Leah looked at me thoughtfully. "He does wake up in the night a lot, I thought . . ." She changed what she was going to say. I winked at her. "I think you're right, he does have bad dreams."

"Doctor, I just can't stop now, I have work to do, I have to get this mess we just bought back to profitability."

"I've given you my advice, up to you if you follow it."

Leah collected everybody together in my hotel room that night to discuss my future. She put the doctor's point of view with admirable economy.

"This loony of mine is going to kill himself if he goes on working. What are we going to do with him?"

"Oh, now, the doctor didn't say that," I objected, "he said I needed more rest."

My friends seemed to feel Leah's version might be more accurate. Fred came in unexpectedly on my side.

"There might be a problem with him leaving right now. If word gets out on the street that our CEO has taken off for a prolonged rest because he's not fit the stock price will take a big hit. We have several thousand shareholders now, some of which might feel cheated. We could get involved in some messy litigation which would make things worse."

That induced a thoughtful silence. Everyone present owned a substantial amount of stock, so the argument had force to it. Secretly I knew the doctor had the right idea. A long rest sounded pretty good. I came up with a compromise.

"Try this. Fred, can you spare a couple of months full time for us?"

"I'd have to ask Harold, but I don't see why not. He has a stake in this too. What do you have in mind?"

"When we dive into SQV Joe is going to have his work cut out starting the Finder business line development, and I expect we'll need him to look at the viability of the other businesses SQV has been spending money on. William has a full time job with the legal affairs of this tottering financial structure we're propping up. And we need to elect a proper board of directors, with outside members, minority stockholder representatives, all that. Mike should be working on strategic planning so we have some guide to what we do with all these divisions SQV has. If you and I go through SQV getting them started toward profitability I could take off on a world cruise ostensibly to visit the countries we expect to do business with, while you implement the short term plans we come up with. If I'm fit enough to operate as CEO when we get back there's no problem, if not I step down as CEO and remain as chairman of the board. If we're profitable, for real, not by cooking the books, no shareholder is going to object."

Leah surprised all of us by bursting into tears. "What ever is the matter," I asked, hugging her while she sobbed.

When she calmed down she explained through the handkerchief I was mopping her face with.

"You must really be sick. You never ever said anything about stepping down before. Oh shit . . . "

She sat down and sobbed quietly to herself. I wasn't the only one who might be entitled to a spell of posttraumatic stress syndrome.

My board told me what I was going to do. Two weeks, then I left if they had to carry me. Leah grabbed my telephone to look up world cruises.

"Wow, here's one. Forty-five days touring the hidden places of the mysterious east that tourists seldom see, reasonable too. We can go first class for less than . . . I'm not going to tell you how much."

"See if there's one two weeks from now, as near as you can get," Joe told her, "and no arguments."

There wasn't one in two weeks, but we could leave from New York in twenty-two days. Leah with her advisory panel, Mary, Roxana, and Celestine, disappeared to Paris to select clothes for forty-five days of cruising. I warned her even a first class cabin didn't have room for a different outfit for every day. Fred promised to make sure I didn't overwork while they were gone.

Chapter 26

Fred and I descended on the remains of SQV as soon as I had rested. One pleasure I had anticipated was denied me. The Group VP had simply stopped coming to work the day after we announced the closing of the New York office, I presume because his friends there warned him what was coming. We marched into the group headquarters building, took the elevator to the top floor. The offices on this floor were not quite as extravagant as those in New York, but definitely not Spartan. The secretary at the desk outside the VP's office looked more like a worker and less like an expensive hooker than the one in New York. She had her purse and some bags piled on the desk. I introduced myself.

"I'm your new boss, and this is my keeper, Fred Cary."

"Yes, sir. May I go now?"

"Go? Where are you going?"

"Aren't I fired?"

I read her name from the plate on her desk. "Miss Andersen, if I want to fire you I'll tell you so. I'd appreciate it if you'd put your things away and act as Fred and my secretary at least until we find out if we suit each other. In any case, unless you've done something to merit firing I would give you the opportunity of finding another spot in the organization."

"Oh," she said, "I heard you were going to fire everybody as soon as you got here."

"Then you're first job is to call round the grapevine and let the organization know that the Mela Corporation plans to run this group just as it is. When we understand it we will have to make some changes because we prefer to make a profit, but that doesn't mean we're going to have any wholesale firings."

"Yes sir," she said brightening up.

"Oh, that reminds me. This organization seems to be spread out over acres and acres of real estate. I'm barely out of a wheelchair. Would you be kind enough to get me a golf cart or something to get around in?"

We went on into the office. Single door, no priceless works of art on the walls, relatively modest furniture but plenty of space for two. "Fred, I suggest we share this office, then we'll know what each other is doing, OK?"

He agreed, so I told our new secretary to get the desk taken away and two smaller ones substituted. We used the armchairs grouped round a low table in a corner. I liked it better than a desk. Next we sent for the Finance Director, bookkeeper in other words. He appeared tight-lipped clutching a briefcase. "Come in, come in, sit down."

"I'd rather stand," he said.

"Let me guess," Fred told him, "you think you're here to be fired."

"Well, er, yes. Aren't you firing all the management?"

"Sit down and let's talk about it. Jim, isn't it?"

He sat on the edge of the armchair.

"Tell us, why does this group not make money?"

"Ah. On paper it does, but there's a negative cash flow. Our military contracts almost all lose money, the whole thing is supported by one or two old Air Force production jobs on which we make it up. Then we have all these mystery development projects which never seem to come to anything. I've worried about it for years, but the management wanted it that way."

"Do you sign off on new bids?" I asked.

"Well yes, but under protest on a lot of them."

"Right, here are some new instructions. If anybody wants to argue send them to me. You are not to sign off on any bid or proposal that you're not personally convinced will make a profit. Will that help?"

"Yes sir, thank you."

"Now, what can we do about these mystery projects?"

"Damned if I know," he answered. "They're all over the place, not under any one manager or in one place. When I've tried to look into some of them I'm told they're classified and I don't need to know."

"Right," Fred took over, "get someone in your office to make a list of them with the name of the reporting manager for each one. If we can't get at them wholesale we'll look into one at a time."

Miss Andersen appeared "Excuse me sir, it's my usual lunch time. May I go now or would some other time be more convenient?"

"We'll all call it lunch time. Is it far to the cafeteria?"

"There's an executive dinning room," she informed us. "That's in this building."

"Maybe, but I want to eat in the cafeteria. Is my golf cart ready?"

So Fred and Jim and I rode in style the few hundred yards to the cafeteria. Jim, he admitted, had never been in it before. We stood in line with trays like everyone else, quite awkward with a stick, not enough hands. Nobody paid any attention to us, they might have known my name but the face hadn't been in the news much. We sat at the end of a long table listening to the sound of the place. The talk sounded worried, subdued. I hoped the grapevine would improve that as the word spread I wasn't an ogre after all. The tables filled up steadily. Half way through my soup-and-salad special combo a woman came by and asked, "Is this seat taken?"

I looked up and she saw my face. Now everyone paid attention to us. She screamed and dropped her tray. "Well, well, well," I said cheerfully, "if it isn't Judith. Haven't seen you since Paris. The seat isn't taken, you're welcome to sit there when you get another lunch. This afternoon report to my office, the Group VP office, I want to talk to you."

She scuttled away but didn't come back to sit with us. People with mops came to clear the mess, and the hum of conversation returned to normal. I think they assumed the tray dropped first and the scream came second. After all I didn't look scary, did I?

My companions wanted to know what the devil that was all about. I said the story could only be told in private, not suitable for publication. Jim wandered off to start his new life, better off I thought knowing as little as possible about the tangled history of the Mela Corporation. I explained it to Fred on the way back to our office.

In the afternoon we sent for the personnel manager, known to the world as The Human Resources Director. He tried to explain the organization chart for all these people. When he got through I turned to Fred, "Do you understand all that?"

"No," he answered," Do you?"

"No. I think there's at least one layer of management too many, and there's divided responsibility for profitability of the projects." I turned to the personnel manager. "Please devote your full time to suggesting a reorganization to solve those two problems with a minimum disruption to the workers. While you're about it, check which of the surplus management layer are entitled to early retirement. Perhaps you'll be ready to lay out a preliminary plan for us to work on by tomorrow afternoon?"

He didn't think that gave him enough time. Fred and I did.

When he'd gone Fred and I looked at each other. "Not a keeper," we agreed.

Our Miss Andersen announced that a person was here to see me, said I'd sent for her. "Come in, Judith," I called.

She came in carrying her purse and a bag of lumpy things with a speech to make. "Just get it over with, don't gloat."

Really, it got tiresome, everyone I met thought I was firing them.

"You," I told her, "are much too useful to fire. That would be a waste of talent. Come here and sit down, I've got a job for you."

She edged gingerly into a chair, keeping well away from me.

"Would I be correct in thinking you report to the security organization somewhere?" She nodded. "Good. Tell your boss you're on assignment for me. I want you to put your skills to work to find out, if you don't already know, who gave the orders that got Leah and Judy and me hurt. Then I want to know everything about them, weakness, strength, credit rating, hobbies, sexual preferences. When I've got all that I'll decide what to do next. Do you know the names now?"

She shook her head. "I got my instructions from a lot lower down."

"I think the former CEO and the Group VP are the prime suspects, but that's for you to find out."

She thought about it for a moment. "I don't suppose I can resign, can I?"

"Why certainly," I beamed at her, "Of course you can. There might be some personal problems though. Getting another job for example. References you know. Then some people might resent your refusing to help undo the damage you had a hand in. Last time I heard Joe mention your name he said something about strangling with his bare hands, don't know how he'll feel about it. Poor Judy, I take the hurt to her personally, I might get upset too. But you make your own decision about it."

"Yes, that's what I thought." She looked down at her hands. "We had you figured completely wrong, for a playboy, nothing to worry about. Now I find you're a really rotten bastard."

"Why, thank you Judith, I take that as a high compliment coming as it does from a master. Give me regular progress reports, not in writing."

When she'd gone Fred looked at me speculatively. "I think she has you taped. You are a rotten bastard. A good quality in a CEO."

"Right. I've had enough sitting in this office, let's go on a tour of the place and see how it looks. Miss Andersen, Get someone from security to escort us please, plain clothes."

We set off in my private transport wandering through the labyrinthine collection of buildings. I picked one at random. We strolled unannounced through the halls looking in offices and laboratories. It didn't seem like a hive of activity. Very calm and relaxed rather. I stopped at one office in which the occupant had fallen asleep leaning back in his easy chair, snoring softly.

"What department are we in?" I asked the security person.

"Model 53, a classified Air Force satellite program."

"Would you be kind enough to find the project manager and ask him to step over here to see me? With no other conversation please."

A few minutes later a man came steaming up with a complaint. "Now who the hell are you, and what do you want on my project?"

"I'm the CEO and Chairman of the Board of the corporation you work for. Is sleeping beauty there," I pointed with my stick, "one of your responsibilities?"

"Oh, sorry, I didn't know. Won't you come down to my office to talk?"

"No, answer the question."

"Er, I suppose so. I'll get his section leader, shall I?"

"No. If that man doesn't have enough work to keep him awake lay him off or transfer him to somewhere he's needed. Make an appointment with my secretary to give me a complete cost and schedule review of your project. Bring your supervisor. Soon, tomorrow would be good."

He tried to justify himself, but Fred said "Soon," and we left him wringing his hands and muttering to himself. I thought that building would now be full of people diligently working, or pretending to, so we moved on to another.

We dived into one labeled 'B16' which made me wonder how many there could be altogether. The middle of this one had windows so we could look in as if into an aquarium. Strange fish indeed swam there. Rows of drafting tables with shirtsleeved individuals bent over them drawing. "Fred," I whispered, "do you think we're in a time warp? Have we got back to the twentieth century? Have you ever seen anything like this?"

Fred turned to our guide. "I know," the guide said, "fetch the department manager." Smart alec.

A little old man came trotting up. "Yes gentlemen, what can I do for you?"

Fred took a turn as the rotten bastard. "This is the CEO of the Mela Corporation, the new owners. We'd like to know what's going on here. Where are the CadCam machines? Why are these men drawing with pencils?"

"Oh, we do the basic design work on the machines, but they don't turn out real quality drawings. We redraw the designs by hand so we have something to be proud of. We've got vellums stored for every mechanical design the company has ever turned out. Quite a remarkable collection. Works of art they are."

I could see turning this place profitable would be quite a big job. Fred took me back to the hotel. He said that was enough for one day.

Chapter 27

There was a CadCam section hidden in the organization of course, run by a bright but frustrated young man. He suddenly became the design department manager when the fossil who had run it decided to take early retirement. Actually, it wasn't early, he should have retired years before. Our temporary office in Torrance moved into the transformed SQV building, now Mela Corporation headquarters. Fred and Mike and I spent hours coming up with a first step reorganization, which generated some more early but overdue retirements. A few frustrating sessions with the Human Resources Director convinced us the organization would run smoother without him so we set a management search firm looking for a new personnel manager. Our overhead looked a lot better in a matter of days, though productivity suffered while the new organization settled down. Joe got the job of going through the list of weird projects and striking off those that didn't make any sense. He took to walking about the plant muttering "no, no, no . . ." under his breath. Then we had to think about the other important element of the business, the customers.

All but two Air Force contracts were losing money, though a lot less now our G&A and overhead had got down to reasonable levels. The other two were enormously profitable, even at the old rates. There could be no question in my mind that the customer and SQV management had connived at some sort of fraud against the government. We had to proceed very carefully, because the GAO might just come and ask for the money back on the excess profits, leaving us to swallow all the losses. Jim, our Finance director, one of the people we retained, did a lot of figuring with incomplete information and guesswork as to what more we could accomplish. He concluded we couldn't make money if we charged a reasonable profit on the two winners, because there would still be too many losers. We'd probably had enough capital to stand the loss when the auto group sale closed, but our stockholders might become restive if we announced that the results of our reorganization and cost cutting turned out to be a reduction in cash flow. In the end we reluctantly decided to share this problem with the responsible Air Force general, whose career wouldn't be enhanced by a GAO audit of his command.

The fewer people the better in this meeting, so Fred and I met with the general in his office at Space Command. General MacIntire was a fatherly, very un-military person. Once we were settled in what passes in the Air Force for easy chairs he opened the conversation by setting off in the wrong direction.

"I suppose you fellows have come to talk me into giving you some more business," he said with an affable smile.

I felt quite sorry to disappoint him. "Er, not exactly general. We've come to talk to you about certain peculiarities in the funding of the projects we've already got."

I watched his face closely, looking for clues as to how much he knew about what was going on. A man with as red a face as his couldn't turn pale, but he tried. Ah, so. He knows all about it. "Peculiarities? What do you mean, are you hinting there are irregularities in our contracting with SQV?"

"Let me be frank general, just between us. We make an excessive profit on Model 53 and White Tiger, and lose money on all the rest. In the last week we've taken thirty points out of our G&A and overhead, but it isn't enough to make the losers profitable and it means our profits on the winners are going from excessive to ridiculous. It's only a matter of time before DCAS or the GAO notice, then where will we all be?" These classified programs have all sorts of odd names, and neither Fred nor I knew what either project did.

"You guys had to rock the boat, didn't you? I was afraid of something like this when you took SQV over. I'll tell you why we did it. We can't get some important development programs funded because we can't convince Congress we need them. The two programs you make money on are favorites with Congress, they never question the estimates for them. We've been getting the same budget for them for years, long after the development finished. Now they're routine production jobs, I should think you do make money on them. And you're supposed to fund the others we want done out of the profits."

We sat and digested this for a moment. "Yes, I guessed it might be something like that," I told him, "but it can't go on. Mela stands to lose a lot of money we can't afford if this becomes public, but your organization is at much more risk. I wouldn't care to be the one who explains it all to a Congressional committee."

Neither would he. Fred had been thinking about it while we talked. "How much control do you have over DCAS, or whoever is the independent contract review authority?"

"Theoretically none," the general answered, "what has that got to do with it?"

"Suppose Mela offered to reduce all your contract prices proportionally to our new rates, would that trigger a more penetrating look into what's going on?"

"Fred, what good would that do?" I asked, because while I could see it didn't change our cash flow, it didn't seem to solve anything.

"It would cut the actual value of the excess profit down considerably, but more important we'd all look like such good guys that I thought maybe nobody would think to look what we were hiding. Then as the losing contracts run out we can either regretfully let them die, or perhaps we can come up with some way to make them at least breakeven. Also, when the whole operation is profitable and our new business line gets going possibly some of the development you want might be done as research by Mela, without a contract. But can you fend off any officious person who wants to know more than is good for him?"

In the old days of course risky R&D got done on 'cost plus' contracts which limited the amount one could lose on them. This practice died out when Congress got fed up with the fact that it didn't limit how much the government could lose on them. The government however retains the right to recover 'excess' profits from all contractors, so they can't lose.

The strain almost made me giggle when it came to my mind that recovering a nuclear bomb in a brightly-lit harbor might be easier than what we were trying to do here. I judged that the chances of someone going to a penal colony, or the military equivalent, were about the same. The sensation of whirling round and round seemed to me quite pleasant. I leaned my head back and closed my eyes to enjoy it. I came to in a wheelchair in the charge of two orderlies on my way out of the building, preceded by Fred muttering about what Leah was going to say when she saw the state I was in. It all struck me as very funny, all these silly people, didn't they know we were all going to be thrown off the earth by the whirling? See, they're all tilted by it. I must have dozed off for a minute, because the next thing I knew I lay on a hard table in the doctor's office with wires hooked to me. The whirling I had enjoyed so much had stopped.

"Ah, we're awake, are we? Perhaps now we'll take my advice, complete rest for a considerable time," he turned to someone standing behind him, "and take that damn telephone away from him. Don't give it back for at least a month."

"Oh, good, Leah, I'm glad you're here. What did Fred agree to? I missed the last bit, went to sleep for some reason."

She came up and hit me. "You are impossible, you're not even going back to the hotel. We are going to live in your beach house until the cruise ship leaves. The hell with what Fred agreed to, leave it to him, that's what he's here for. Enough is enough, it took all that time for me to make up your mind to marry me, now I don't want to lose you after all that trouble."

Of course I couldn't really just drop out. Mike came up with the way to keep the street from realizing the Mela CEO had what used to be called a 'nervous breakdown.' Thoroughly rested, carefully dressed, and covered with elaborate makeup I taped a bright cheery interview for CNBC. Watching it next day it convinced even me. I told them how well the takeover went, how our cost cutting had already reduced our total overhead thirty percent with more to come, how morale and productivity were on the rise after the initial shock of the reorganization. Now we were looking ahead to the opening up of new markets for the commercial versions of the Finder technology. As our team was well able to manage the slimmed down existing operations I felt my place was to introduce Mela to the potentially enormous customer base of the Far East. The interviewer had to ask penetrating questions for his audience.

"Didn't firing all the existing SQV management disrupt the organization? How are you going to make the operation profitable after that?"

"No, that's just a rumor. We retained all the management talent we need. I'd mention in particular our CFO who had been with SQV for many years and we hope will continue with Mela for many more. We did eliminate a layer of quite unnecessary management, but not by wholesale firing. We did a careful reorganization, treated people as individuals. The organization will change more as we grow into new product lines under Dr Jenkin's guidance, but we expect to be hiring rather than laying off." Sounds good, doesn't it?

"Did your customer relations suffer from the changes? What does the Air Force think of all this?"

"I'm glad you asked. We're getting an award from General MacIntire for voluntarily reducing the price of all our contracts with him for a saving to the taxpayer of several million dollars, while at the same time increasing our cash flow. SQV had become uncompetitive in some areas, we have or will shortly reverse this so our military business will rise in amount, but fall in relation to our total as our new commercial lines come on stream. I have instructed our CFO that he is not to approve new bids unless he is convinced of their potential profitability. In other words, we don't offer 'loss leaders' any more."

"Mela stock at two hundred is at a rather high multiple of earnings, would you advise our viewers to buy it?"

"I'm not in the business of giving financial advice, your viewers should be guided by their own research. As to the multiple, I think anyone who has seen the sonic holograph in operation will value Mela as a growth high-tech company. In that light our stock's considerably undervalued."

"Do you plan a stock split in the near future?"

"It wouldn't be proper for me to comment on that, though I would say I'd rather the share price put it in the reach of the average small investor."

"There has been talk on the street that you were incapacitated by some injuries, can you comment on that?"

"I certainly can. I survived a cowardly assassination attempt made, I believe, to interfere with the conduct of our takeover offer. I needed some repair surgery, but as you can see I'm completely recovered. In any case, the attempt failed in both its aims."

By the end of the interview I knew I was giddy and covered with sweat but on TV I looked healthy and confident. By the close Mela stock was at two hundred and twenty.

First class on a real ocean cruise, not a weekend singles party, is an experience not to be missed. That's if you don't mind spending an average person's year's salary on it. I rested most of the time during the day, to save energy for the nights. Leah said I'd wear myself out, I said what a way to go. I really did talk to some people in China, enough to justify the trip as a business expense. The IRS of course is tiresome about things like that, but that's what lawyers are for.

Leah enjoyed the Captain's table for meals, showing off her diamonds and Paris gowns. Mind you, there were some worthy rivals there, but I don't think anybody had earrings to match hers. The really spectacular jewelry displays appeared on older women, so Leah's looked better.

I met some interesting people on the trip, heads of businesses, financiers. Very educational to listen to. They discreetly inquired about the real prospects for Mela and the Finder. I could honestly tell them it was 'the invention of the century' whose whole potential even Dr Jenkins had not fully explored. These conversations tended not to last for long, because Leah took strong objection to my talking business when I was supposed to be resting. True to her instructions she wouldn't give me my phone back. I didn't even know were our stock had got to.

One bit of business did get transacted, only I didn't know what it was. A ship's officer approached us with a telegram as we sat in deckchairs enjoying the sun and breeze. I put my hand out for it but Leah got it first with an "Oh no you don't." She read it thoughtfully then looked at me and said "Say yes." In a relaxed mood watching the sea slide by of course I said "Anything you want, my love."

"Just send 'He approves' for a reply please."

In forty-five days I put on quite a lot of weight, got a tan, almost forgot Mela though I had my scars to remind me of SQV. Leah complained that if I got any healthier one woman wouldn't be enough, she'd have to get help. I pretended to think about it, asked who she had in mind. I can't imagine what the cabin attendant thought of the aftermath of the pillow fight that resulted. Flimsy things, who'd have thought they had real feathers in them?

Chapter 28

I noticed the improvement in the tone of the former SQV as soon as I arrived at the headquarters building. I sensed a brisk purpose about the offices, saw people walking quickly or typing diligently at their computers. People smiled when they said 'good morning' to me. My management team had evidently accomplished a lot in the month and a half I'd been gone. I'd met with them all the night before to get briefed on the situation, including the five-for-one stock split that I'd agreed to from the cruise ship. I would have approved it if I'd been asked, so I suppose in spirit I had.

Miss Andersen had kept my day reasonably free, except for lunch in the executive dinning room with the number one candidate for the new Human Resources Director. My desk now sported a voice-actuated teleconferencing screen, connected only to the executive offices but planned, she said, to be extended to the whole plant.

"Who is responsible for this improvement?" I asked her.

"Oh, Mr. Cary is. He said 'this organization is going to be dragged by the scruff of its neck into the twenty-first century.' He had a lot to say about antiquated methods." She giggled, "He told one department manager to install steam engines, he should feel right at home with the technology."

Excellent, Fred had laid the foundation for me to look like Mr. Nice Guy in comparison, not the image I had left with. My secretary had two people who wanted to see me. I told her to let Judith Parker come as soon as convenient, but couldn't remember any Mr. Jones I would want to see.

"He said to say you might remember him as agent Jones, you'd want to see him. He's been coming to the lobby and calling all the time you've been gone. He wouldn't believe you weren't here."

"Ah, now I know who he is. Have him wait while I see Miss Parker, send him in when I buzz."

Judith dutifully appeared that afternoon. "Come in, sit down," I told her, "have you found the head of the serpent?"

"Head? Oh, I see. Yes, I think so. You wouldn't believe what I had to do to get all this for you."

"And I don't want to know. Who's at the bottom of it?"

"You were right, the group VP gave the orders, through Security. Do you want the names in Security?"

"I will, but the principals first. Who else?"

"The corporate headquarters knew all about it. All of them wanted to run up the stock price by claiming they had the Finder in development. The stock hadn't done anything for years, they were worried about a takeover. They didn't worry enough, did they?"

I pressed the buzzer. Miss Andersen ushered in the former agent Jones.

"Oh god, " Judith moaned, "what's he doing here?"

"I don't know, come in Jones and tell us, what are you doing here?"

"You got me fired from the Bureau, they put the word out so I can't get a job anywhere, I've tried. I thought maybe you might . . . "

"We'll see, sit down and listen. Judith has explained who the SQV principals were in the round of kidnapping, arson, and assassination we were subject to. What I don't understand is how the FBI got involved. Do you know?"

"I got my instructions from the station chief, don't know where his came from."

"Judith, do you know?"

She shook her head. "I haven't done anything about that branch, you didn't ask."

"What's this man's name?"

"The bureau chief? Kreutzer."

"Now, you want a job, do you?"

Judith interrupted. "Don't do it, he'll give you something terrible to do, you'd be better off pumping gas."

"See," I pointed out to him, "I have loyal dedicated employees who love their jobs, just like the FBI. You'll be right at home."

He looked shaken "What would you want me to do?"

"It's payback time for poor Judy, for Leah, for William's leg, for the torching of the Mermaid, for the scars on my chest, for my burned Mercedes, and I expect for a lot of other people I've never heard of. We're going to kill this serpent."

Both of them protested they weren't going to do murder for me.

"No, I don't want anybody killed. I'm much more vindictive than that. Jones, do you want a job or not?"

"Short of murder, yes."

"You'll be sorry," Judith whispered to him.

"Right, Judith, leave me the reports on the people we're going to destroy, then take Jones and get him taken on in the section where you work. Tell personnel to grade him by his paper qualifications for now, like any other new hire. Then I want to know where Kreutzer gets his orders, I don't mean in the Bureau, I mean the connection with SQV. When I've read your reports I'll give you new instructions."

So far, except for the Air Force, I'd not paid much attention to the important part of the business, the customers. "Miss Andersen, would you get the Contracts Manager in here to see me?"

He turned up panting, evidently with a nice appreciation for the hazards of an interview with the CEO. "Who are our important customers," I asked him once we were seated.

"The only large single customer is Space Division, the rest are kind of scattered. What do you have in mind?"

"I want to go visit the management of some customers, find out what we have to do to become number one in each of our businesses. If I could puzzle out what our businesses are."

"Yes, well one of the problems with that is the amount of business we have in the black, that is so highly classified that even the name of the customer is 'secret.' Until you get an appropriate security clearance I can't discuss them."

"Well, what lines do we have with big name customers that you can talk about?"

"We build the chassis and payload support module for some Lockheed-Martin commercial satellites, and we make a standard telemetry system for Boeing. You could talk to them."

"We, you and I. Set up meetings with the highest level you can, we'll go on a tour. Include any other places you think would be valuable, even small ones so I can get a feel for our image. And what to do about it. Perhaps you'd be kind enough to set up a meeting for us with whoever the responsible people are for those two projects. I'd like to know if there's anything I can offer to make the customers love us."

"Oh, right, yes sir."

I'd made somebody's day.

I buzzed Miss Andersen. "Come in and help me with a problem," I told her.

She came and I directed her to an easy chair. She sat warily.

"I'm going on a sort of sales trip, to LM at Sunnyvale and Boeing at Seattle. My wife is going to be very upset with me if I get overtired, walk too much, don't get enough rest. How do you suggest I go about it? And would you explain why you look so nervous?"

"Um, it's .. The man who was here before, you see . . . He . . . " She stopped with a deep blush.

"Ah, so that's it. Let me assure you, your relations with me are strictly business. I don't want to know what your relations with the former group VP were, but that's how it is with me. At work you are my personal assistant, no more and no less. Outside work I don't know you. Now in that light, how about my trip?"

"Thank you very much for telling me, I've been worrying about what I was expected to do. I suppose you'd use the company jet, that's what it's for. Then I'll get a limo to meet you everywhere you stop."

"*Company jet?* We've got a jet? How the hell much is that costing?"

"I'm sure I don't know, quite a lot I should think. You might as well use it, otherwise it's sitting around idle."

When I broke the news of the trip to Leah the plans changed abruptly. "Just you wait," she informed me, "tomorrow I'm coming to work with you to talk to your Miss Andersen. Let you loose on a four day trip up the West Coast indeed I won't."

So the contract manager and his wife, and me and my supervisor, went on a much more relaxed trip than I had planned. Formal meetings in the afternoon only, the real business over dinner with the management we were visiting plus wives or significant others, Leah as hostess. An altogether better plan than mine. And highly successful. I'll tell you how the Lockheed-Martin meeting went as a sample. It started unpromisingly.

"I'm afraid you've wasted a trip," I was told, "we're going to put the telemetry package out for new bids. Your price is too high for us, we don't like having to take such big quantities, and there are some bad units we've got problems with."

"I do understand your position, but it isn't a wasted trip. First let me tell you our overhead has been cut by thirty percent, and this will be reflected in your next invoice. On the quantities, I came to suggest you might prefer us to ship just-in-time, so you hold no inventory at all. I'll stock enough to guarantee next day delivery, same day if you're in a bind. Can't understand why we haven't always done it that way. After the overhead cut, what price would convince you to stay with us?"

"I'm afraid we need at least a forty percent total cut for you to be competitive. I'm sure that's too much. Sorry."

What he didn't know is that we would make a profit on these units at less than that, if we rationalized the production and made some design improvements. I glanced at my contract manager. He nodded. I held my hand out. "Shake, it's a deal. Your next invoice will be at sixty percent of our present price, and the price is good for one unit or any other quantity."

The temperature went up considerably. We weren't quite through. "What about defectives?"

"As I don't know what's the matter with them, I don't know how to fix it. Could your people spare the time to work with my engineers if I sent a team to diagnose the difficulty here, where you people can be in on it? That way we can make sure it's not an interface or environmental problem."

"I've asked for that before, never got it."

I took out my trusty pocket communicator. What we used to call a phone. "Hello? Miss Andersen? I need an engineering team to diagnose problems with the telemetry units we sell

Lockheed, right now. Get them on a plane tonight, have them report to Mr." I looked a question at the manager. He gave me a name. "Worthing first thing in the morning. They know which building. They'd better. Tell them they stay until they have a permanent fix, than retrofit every unit that's still available. No charge of course. Call me back to confirm."

"I think we can look forward to a continuing relationship with the Mela Corporation," he announced. A very pleasant dinner we had with him and his wife. We took away the promise of several other bid opportunities.

What we got from the trip wasn't the several million dollars in business we'd salvaged and the new business in the making, because the amounts were actually trivial compared with our gross. The real value lay in the insight it gave me into the long-building problems I'd inherited, and how to fix them.

Next day I found I had a new problem. "A Mr. Kreutzer wants to talk to you for your own good, do you want to?"

I pressed the record button on my telephone. To be strictly legal of course this is supposed to beep every ten seconds to let the caller know he's being recorded. That would be silly, wouldn't it? Spoils the whole idea.

"Yes?"

No preamble from him, an equally terse reply, "You've hired Jones."

A statement I didn't think needed a reply from me. I waited. "Well?" he said.

"Well what Mr. Kreutzer? I'm pretty busy, please get to the point."

"I want to know why you've hired him."

"I don't see any possible reason why I should discuss Mela Corporation personnel policies with you, so I'm not going to. Is that all you have to say?"

"I warn you, don't cross the FBI, we can make things very difficult for you. Just forget the things that happened in the past, don't stir the mud or you'll regret it."

"What things in the past might those be that I'm to forget?" I asked in the hope of getting something good on record.

"You know what I'm talking about, quit while you're ahead."

"You mean kidnapping? Assault? Arson? Attempted murder? Are those the things I should forget?"

"I've warned you," he said and disconnected.

I spent some time re-reading 'The Art of War' to see what Sun-Tzu had to say. In taking on the FBI I needed all the help I could get. His advice to strike swiftly with sufficient force to get a quick victory looked good to me. As did 'assess your own and your enemy's strengths and weaknesses.' My key strength and his weakness lay in the ability to spend a substantial amount of money. His strength lay in the command of a well-trained army, who would apparently do anything they were told, legal or not. His weakness was that he took his orders indirectly from the branch of government in perpetually need of campaign finance money who would stop at nothing to get it.

Next day I gave my personal assistant a challenging assignment. "I need to get to the President." She looked confused. To her I was the president. "Of the United States, but I don't think he'll talk to me direct. I didn't even vote for him. Isn't our senior Senator close to him?"

"That's what he claims, says he can get things done for his state."

"See if you can get the Senator to come for dinner with me next time he's in town, him and his wife. Give as the reason that I'm considering making a contribution to his campaign fund. If they want to know how much say you don't know but you heard something about a half-million dollars."

A week later the Senator and his wife sat to dinner with Leah and I at the Marina Yacht club.

Chapter 29

The Senator looked, in real life instead of television, like a slightly off actor portraying a senator. His mane of white hair so carefully sculpted, his face lined and pale without pancake makeup. His wife had kept better than he, dressed, to my amateur eye, fashionably with some interesting jewelry. Colored stones seemed to be her preference, not my taste. She couldn't keep her eyes off Leah's earrings.

No business at dinner, Leah commanded, we'll have coffee and liqueurs on our yacht, just a few yards down the pier. We'll be private there, and we can enjoy this pleasant evening on the upper deck watching the moon. Once we were settled there the ladies started discussing the relative merits of French vs American designers and I started a delicate approach to the Senator.

"Senator, we at Mela have a small problem which you might be able to help us with, through your friend in the White House. Mela you know employs over ten thousand voters in your district, and if we continue to grow at our present rate that'll soon be twenty thousand. A large proportion of that business is with the government, though I plan for our commercial side to be the one to expand. Our sonic hologram business should contribute substantially to improving the US balance of trade in time. The goodwill of several branches of government is important to us, so if we meet hostility in one we are naturally concerned. A little more brandy?"

"Thank you, yes, very good. I can't interfere in your contracts with the government you know, most of your competitors are in my state too."

"Oh, we wouldn't want you to," I assured him, "all we want is the chance to compete fairly, we don't need help there. No, our problem's with a different branch altogether. May I play a recent telephone conversation for you?"

He looked round to make sure the boats round us were untenanted. "Go ahead."

I pressed the button on my phone to play back the memory stick of Kreutzer's call. "That man, who is he?" he asked when it finished.

"That sir is the LA bureau chief of the FBI, upon whom we rely for our security clearances. What else he may be involved in that the public would be better off not knowing I can't say, but I have incontrovertible proof he's been the principle in at least one vicious kidnapping."

"Are you planning to take this to . . . yes, I see. You can't very well go to the FBI for help, now can you." He chuckled. "What do you want me to do about it, though I don't know what I can do."

"We want as little fuss as possible, certainly don't want a public dispute with the FBI. What I wonder is if Mr. Kreutzer wouldn't be happier in another, perhaps less demanding position, one where he isn't subject to the temptations of the big city. I don't know if there's an FBI bureau in the Aleutian Islands, but if there is it would be ideal."

The Senator found this very amusing, kept repeating 'Aleutian Islands' to himself and laughing. Then he got to the nub of the matter. "Now in theory the FBI is independent, though of course the Chief has some influence with them. There would be certain difficulties in the way of accomplishing what you suggest, amusing as it is. By the way, I thought I heard a mention of campaign contributions, not of course that they would have any bearing on this matter."

"Of course not, but since you bring it up I did plan to get the Mela Corporation to make a substantial gift, 'soft' money of course so it can't go direct to you."

"The amount I heard fell a little short of substantial," he said softly to the moon.

"I don't know what you heard, but even to Mela a million dollars is quite substantial."

"I agree," he said, "I must have been misinformed. I'll let you know how the money should be directed. It's unfortunate that this generosity can only be impersonal, isn't it?"

Well, he didn't bother much about being delicate, did he? I suppose a lifetime of collecting gifts and contributions had hardened him to the sordid details. I had expected the need for a direct bribe so was ready.

"We were wondering Senator, if your good wife could spare us a morning to visit our usual jewelers on Rodeo drive so we could present her with some small token of our appreciation for your attention. I see she is fond of ruby, possibly they might have a trinket she could wear."

"How small?"

"Something she might wear to a State Department dinner."

"I think I could see my way clear to discussing your little difficulty with the Chief. I'd expect if he takes it up you should see results about the end of next week. Tomorrow you said for my wife to visit your jewelers?"

"Yes indeed, and I think we can have a check in the hands of your designee by the end of next week."

"Good, good. Now we've neglected our ladies for too long. This is indeed a delightful spot for relaxing of an evening. Perhaps I should get one."

So we talked of boats and places. Leah described her experiences in the Mediterranean when left in charge of the pilothouse of the Mermaid, the Senators wife shared the time she went on an Eco cruise to places where, as she put it, there weren't any proper toilets and the air was full of biting things. I loaded them into the company limo with a feeling of a good evening's work accomplished.

Leah couldn't hear what had transpired because she had a full-time job entertaining the Senator's wife. "Did we win?" she asked.

"If you call spending a million dollars to get rid of Kreutzer we did, plus we have to buy that woman some rubies. I hope it's worth it."

Next morning I called the jeweler as soon as they opened to lay the groundwork for our visit. After we got through the 'How is M'sieur? And dear Madame?' I told him what I wanted.

"We're bringing the Senior Senator's wife in to buy her a little gift. I gather she likes rubies. I think she may not appreciate the finer points of quality, perhaps will be influenced more by size. I wouldn't put it past the Senator to get it appraised though.

I thought something along the lines of a pendant, but she eyed Leah's earrings all evening. Now I don't want to spend as much as that, so show her things about twenty thousand dollars. Put it on my Paris account, saves sales tax."

"I comprehend, this is perhaps a token of appreciation for some action of the Senator's?"

"Precisely, I'm sure you've handled similar matters before."

"Mais oui, certainment. We will do our best to se the lady is well pleased so the Senator will be amiable, n'est pas?"

The lady was well pleased, though we went over budget quite a bit.

Friday the next week I got a call from the new chief of the LA bureau, assuring me of the goodwill and cooperation of the FBI. "And where has Mr. Kreutzer moved to?" I asked innocently.

"Apparently the President has concerns about security in Alaska, now we have an open border across the Bering Straits. He asked the Bureau to send a senior man to run an office up there. Kreutzer got the honor."

Not as good as the Aleutians, but it would do. Couldn't happen to a better man.

I found time to give Jones and Judith their assignments. I enjoy Judith's asides, most amusing.

"See, I told you not to take the job. He's found something really rotten for you to do."

The former SQV management has been dogged by an extraordinary run of bad luck, almost as if a malignant fate were pursuing them. The ex-CEO's wife left him abruptly and got a most generous settlement in her divorce because some well wisher informed her that her husband kept a teen-age mistress in Pasadena. The details were very convincing, and checking the address indeed found a person living there who matched the description she'd been given. Her husband denied all knowledge of the young lady, insisting throughout the various court proceedings that someone had fabricated the whole story. Nobody believed him. For some reason no reputable company would give him a job in any capacity. He has also had very bad luck with his investments. Generally buying small cap stocks on margin is a risky business, but if you have an enemy in the market with more capital than you do it becomes financial suicide. By a strange coincidence everything he bought became the target of a bear raid, selling short until his margin was wiped out. As soon as he sold out the bears bought back to return the stocks to their original value or higher. His judgement of the value of these stocks was quite good, and my portfolio has benefited appreciably from his misfortunes. His attempt to recoup by buying into a real estate development scheme went sour because the land in question turned out to contain a native American burial ground which they somehow couldn't get permission to move. Most unfortunate. Not however as unfortunate as the fate of the former VP for the SQV Defense and Electronics Group, now part of the Mela Advanced Technology Group.

He had the misfortune to be caught with a large amount of child porn material in his house and car, with evidence he had been mailing it to juniors. He too denied all knowledge of it, claimed it wasn't in his car when he went into the supermarket-someone must have planted the whole thing. A likely story. When his attorney challenged the search warrant the police produced supporting evidence supplied by a concerned citizen who's son had been getting the material regularly. The citizen supplied copies with postmarked wrapping showing the offense had been going on for some time so of course the warrant stood. He committed suicide during the trial, which I thought a pity. His farewell note maintained his innocence, repeated his claim that the whole thing was a malicious fabrication invented to ruin him. Now who would believe a thing like that?

I got the names of all the lower level people who had been involved in the various attempts on our lives and liberty. They work now for the Mela Corporation, in security. Sun-Tzu says "When you capture soldiers, give them responsibilities according to their strengths, take care of them kindly, and they will work for you." I think I have a most loyal and effective security department, Few 'rotten jobs' come their way, but if I ever need a rotten job again I've got the organization for it.

Chapter 30

With these extraneous matters out of the way I could get down to the work of running the Corporation, developing an in-depth management team, all that stuff. It took years, some down times when the Chairman of the Federal Reserve decided we were all enjoying ourselves too much, some up years when everything went right.

Under my leadership Mela has done rather well, if I do say so myself. Joe has been able to attract the best engineering and scientific talent in the world to work under him. We have some really exciting new projects in development. One with great promise is pure science, but worth it for the technological fallout. Joe has a team working on advanced signal processing applied to the synthetic images formed by very large astronomic telescope arrays. I hear a whisper that visible images of planets circling other stars might be just around the corner. Our Medical Devices Division produces a whole line of real-time 3-D sonic imaging systems without of course the hazards and difficulty of radiation based methods. X-rays are almost obsolete as a result. Pre-natal photos are now a big thing with young mothers, printed direct onto micro-lens cards so the image is in 3-D. Myself, I could do without them, but I don't argue with what sells. Mela stock, as you are aware if you were perspicacious enough to buy when it was at 250, has split five-for-one several times. This gave us the currency to make some significant purchases. The new Domestic Information Devices division, formerly Compaq Computer has, I think it's safe to say, a nasty shock in store for Bill Gates. I'll give you a hint–I didn't write this the conventional way by *talking* to the computer.

The Human Resources Director I hired has been a tremendous asset, raising Mela from the old SQV image of the most boring place to work in LA to a model employer. He introduced a day care facility so we could tap into the labor pool of young mothers, something other area firms did years ago. His company sponsored 4-H club for teenage children of employees and the new college scholarship funds will help ensure a continuous supply of eager and talented people for the future. I find most entertaining his battles with our CFO for funds for long range projects like these in competition with the need to show a short-term profit.

Mela bought Mico, Joe's plant in Torrance you remember, to make the basis of our Control Systems Division. Joe used the cash to endow a chair in Theoretical Physics at a predominantly black college.

Even our Defense Systems Division makes a modest profit, less than I'd like but considerably more than the military would like. My limiting the defense business to making only Mil Spec versions of our commercial products had been the key to this. We do not accept government funded research contracts, as we prefer to maintain a proprietary position on every development we undertake. A certain Air Force general refers to this as "having us over a barrel." He exaggerates.

On the whole the people who were involved in our adventures have survived in good order. Except poor Judy. Nothing could give her back all of her mind and her health. She has a medical pension from Mela as, for bookkeeping purposes, a former employee. Leah visits her sometimes but I'm not sure Judy recognizes her. She seems happy enough in her cottage by the Hudson, with a housekeeper and a nurse who looks in every day, for bookkeeping purposes part of our New York sales office.

Pam? I've never seen or heard of her since she walked out of my life in Marseilles. All I know is she returned my car, so I like to think she attained her ambition of settling down to respectability.

I don't need to tell you about Mikel and Natasha, their series of best-selling travel adventure books tells it all. They now have their own Eco tour company, specializing in trips definitely not for the faint hearted.

As to our original group who sat speculating on the existence and nature of sea serpents on the veranda of my Malibu house, now my weekend cottage, we have on the whole done well. Joe is one of the richest black people in America, an honorary doctor at several universities, here and in France. He is much in demand as a speaker at black functions but doesn't have a lot of time to spare for outside engagements. He commutes with Celestine between LA and Paris with side trips to Tokyo, as the Mela Corporation VP for Research and Development. Their three children speak several languages, often simultaneously. Mike, our VP for Strategic Planning, lives with Mary but they have never seen the need to get married. I have a suspicion Mike feels his relationship with her is more secure when she doesn't have a legal claim on any of his modest fortune. William is of course our VP for Legal and Government Affairs, the government in question mostly being the IRS. Blake took no part in our adventures and should have been able to live comfortably on his shares in Mela, but instead the money went to his head somehow, apparently the difference between being well off and being rich encouraged him to what you might call excesses. As far as I know he is not now in a sanatorium, but has spent a good part of his time in one recovering from the effects of too much. Of everything.

My dear wife is active in local politics, where she is very popular and not I think only because of her generous contributions to worthy causes. I don't know how she finds time as well as raising our two hellions. Don't know who they get it from. When they get too much, their honorary grandmother in Madison takes them for a few days, from which they come back temporarily better behaved. Mildred claims she enjoys having them. She is not fooled for an instant by my daughter Celestine's air of girlish innocence.

For myself, there's rich and there's very rich, and I do like very rich. I would like to say I was well, but the effects of a bullet in the chest tend to be permanent. Running and cycling are beyond me, but I put in a full week's work. Most weeks.

I donated the Wilmington Steam Navigation Tug 16, a.k.a. Mela Mermaid, a.k.a. Belle Celestine, to a French university archeological department, complete with the prototype Finder. They stripped out the custom designer cabins to substitute a dormitory with bunks and the usual coed bathroom. Rather un-French I thought.

And did we ever find the sea serpent? I'm really not sure. We do have a recording from the Finder we never share with anyone. It shows some very large animal just sliding out of the picture with a saucy flip of its tail. Wriggling, as Dr Joseph 'I told you guys so' Jenkins points out, up and down. And good luck to it whatever it may be.

THE END